Helios

By

James Lawless

LAFAYETTE, TENNESSEE
deepreadpress@gmail.com

First Deep Read Press Edition.

Published in the United States of America

Edited by: Angie Novoa

Cover Design by: Kim Gammon

ISBN: 978-1-954989-59-7

Published by:

DEEP READ PRESS

Lafayette, Tennessee

www.deepreadpress.com

deepreadpress@gmail.com

For Declan Kiberd

Helios

1

On a sweltering afternoon with the temperature hitting 40 plus Paul Guilfoyle boards a train at Atocha station in Madrid and heads east. He arrives at the small coastal town of C—, and after a little enquiring he secures from a matronly *cubana* the rental of a modest one-bedroom apartment on an upper floor with a commanding view of the sea and the streets of the town below.

Climbing the narrow stairs, his bags and accoutrements knock against side walls as sweat forms little oceans under his oxters. Paul's robust nature and large hands had him called upon for the heavy lifting to be done in the monastery, leading the lifting now to be easy. He unpacks from his battered cream cardboard suitcase which his mother had bought for him in Clery's of Dublin, a noted supplier of clerics' clothes, for five pounds, on the day of his leaving home for the Brotherhood and which he had guarded with affection all the years. He hangs his clothes neatly, checking the creases in his pants, in the narrow teak wardrobe and on the little table beside his bed he places his navy leatherbound diary, some books on art and his (unexpurgated) *Stories of Ancient Greece and Rome* which before leaving Dublin he had seen in the window of a bookshop in Nassau Street and congratulated himself on being able to succumb at last to any natural predilection. *Not those books, Brother. They are not the books to read. We need to focus our minds on uplifting literature. Words that will enhance us. Words that the Saviour would like us to hear.*

He wonders where to position the potted plant which also he had brought from Dublin and which he is glad to be relieved of, for it had proved awkward in its transportation and he marvels that it survived its wrapping in an aeroplane hold. He steadies the plant, a Robinia, a treasured gift from his old mentor Brother Marías, under the running tap for several moments, straightening out its feathery foliage and eventually places it on the small balcony where he can hear the seagulls screeching and smell the salt carried on a warm breeze from the nearby beach. To the west is a high mountain and a forest of tall cedars and larch and pine with eucalyptus and some venerable oaks. And to his right, opulent gate-locked villas.

As the evening is still young he slips into a fresh shirt and walks to the sandy beach to cool down after his journey.

Perhaps it is more of a physical infatuation, pure physical desire, seeing her upside down bottom doing a somersault flip that does something to him. It is Eros coming into action as her black bikini rear expands delectably into the wide womanly curves that men can only marvel at. She dives, illuminating the seat, the centre of fantasy and desire. That bottom freezes like a still picture and becomes ingrained in his consciousness as the trigger for *la petite mort*, the shedding and ultimate death (what is that moment?) of all mankind, like the flower, like it is the way to follow the predestined path. All very well, one may be tempted to say, but physical desire of such magnitude at his age! Touching seventy. What is he to do as he reflects on his own mortality fast approaching, the age of forgetfulness and dodderiness, an old man to be indulged or ignored, posing no danger to child or beast or woman. But such an age has its advantages, bestowing a freedom to express the inner thoughts— all those deemed impurities formally proscribed by the institution— which younger men keep bottled up, fearing curtailment perhaps by those strident misandrists who are forever pontificating in the media these days. That is why the bucks may be jealous of him when they express moral outrage at his now newly-found unrestrictive utterances. It has happened when he'd be free with his thoughts in his local pub near his flat in Drumcondra, which he had recourse to occasionally after leaving the order, where he would smile inwardly at the pouting and posturing of the morally convention-bound.

What age is the source of this erotic feeling? Somewhere in her late thirties perhaps, forty at the most, so maybe not too young but in prime, if that is the word. Is this infatuation lust, something that should have faded with the body? But what of love? There is no such thing as love (except for charity of course, another of our conditionings). If it exists at all, it lies in recollection like all knowledge as Kierkegaard would have us believe. If it is merely recollection, what has he to look forward to? But no, it is a manufactured concept, a construct for our conventional world and a... there she goes out of the water now and that cant of the hips constantly drawing one on. The body and the eye, what does the eye see? Does the eye distort. Is its lens accurate? What he is beholding, is it real? If she were to move another way would it dampen the ardour?

He shuffles uncomfortably with his slight erection, pleased to have it, so long since, almost stuck to the plastic seat of the beach bar mere yards away from the object of his gaze, drawing attention to himself in his long cotton pants, provoking a quizzical underneath-the-sunglasses glance of a bronzed male sunbather.

She is talking now to a young girl reclining on a sunbed beside her. Is the young girl her daughter perhaps, and where is the husband? One is tempted to speculate. She speaks as he sees her full lips move to that putative daughter, not yet quite at puberty with the little jutting pimples of breasts like pinpricks through the cerise of her taut swimsuit.

He had walked in the early morning two days before he departed for Spain under a gunmetal grey sky along the canal bank near his Dublin flat seeking the sun, and he thought from her tears the dandelion (of which there were many growing haphazardly about) is born, resembling the sun when in flower and the moon when in seed, and the stars are its leaves at its base. He was musing on the letter from the Mater hospital left unopened on the kitchen table—about his prostate condition, he didn't want to know, not yet— when he spotted a mourning wreath in the still water.

And the next day he went to the canal again and the flowers of the wreath were all split and scattered on the bank. The swans, some passer-by said, but he wondered. And later that evening with his Derwent pencil he tried to capture the two images of the wreath, before and after its destruction.

Paul Guilfoyle was one who did not deviate. Up to this point that is. And, as for that letter, it can stay there unopened until he returns from completing his life. He had kept to the celibate rule despite the racking in his head and, like Saint Augustine, battled with his natural impulses, for he thought that was what he was supposed to do, what he had signed up for. He did not know of loopholes or falsification or sophistry. But the sex scandals, when they struck wide in the open and the multi-paedophilia cases that became exposed in congregations and orders, actually did him a favour, for they lifted that huge burden of responsibility and conscience-wrestling off his shoulders. He could turn his back now on the Church with impunity and, like so many lay people, could feel justified in so doing, and no one in the outer world would think him remiss. A failed cleric no longer carries a stigma, no more, no less, than a failed showband singer. One may enquire why he did not get out earlier. But certain things remained within him, things he could not shake off, ingrained in him like a meditative disposition or turning the other cheek and that pressing sense of seeking justice for the world.

The admired lady frowns towards her daughter who is excitedly showing off her underwater feats. But the lady has had enough. She emerges, and her breasts peep in their revelatory fullness from the blue of the water, only half cupped by her bikini top, her gypsy black hair dripping in sensual streaks on her olive skin. Oh to touch, as one who was starved all his life, the survivor of a famine, to go near as she moves and the bend, the delicious bend as she stoops to put on her flipflops. Such an overpowering life-giving urge takes hold of him like the bull rush to the cow, the runting deer to the fawn, the march hare to the doe, but he knows man is prevented from following this natural gravitation and constricted on the so-called civilised path. The husband is banished to where, or was he the culprit having an affair, a falling out, packing his bags and vamoosing? But who can tell? The alluring element in the lady could be a veneer and belie a cantankerousness or bitchy nature. However, in the purely organic world, words are supernumerary.

The lady is drying herself now with a yellow towel from which Helios beams, and why would he not, coming into contact as he does with those delectable parts? She looks towards her daughter laughing by the shoreline. The daughter is talking to a boy who has all the shyness and clumsiness of youth evidenced by his pustular gestures and shoulder shrugging and occasional downward glances to the sands formed by the receding waves as if their depths held answers to the age old conundrum. A self-conscious boy developing into his growing form, wondering what it will be, what lies in front of his skinny torso and bony legs through the route of the forest of acne and facial and pubic and the prayed-for chest hairs. What will give him confidence or take his confidence away at this formational stage of his life? Will he, like Paul, be taken in by some ideology or other? Or will he be pragmatic and see the world as unveiled like some of today's shrewd authors and, instead of alcohol, drink copious cups of tea and go to bed early and live a petty bourgeois life? Paul at fourteen. A postulant, a raw recruit. For what? Signing up on the ship of folly to satisfy somebody, some nebulous leader with a beard. Not all men who wear beards are Messiahs. Now does he know.

And yet his everbleaching facial hair he finds himself reluctant to shed. Years and life's experience dictating acceptance or rejection in the social spectrum. The world makes him, not he the world. Only in senescence can the latter happen because then you already have been made, all the parts have been assembled and put together in some place in the cosmos of your body distorted or not, so there is nothing left now, nothing to fear for you are already formed with not a thing remaining to be achieved. At seventy you must make do with your own fallible devices for that is to be human. You don't have to impress anyone anymore and you no longer have to care if nobody impresses you. So that former natural shyness reinforced by the encouraged demureness of the cloister he can cast aside now. For he has nothing to lose, not at this stage of his unfurling. Except his virginity of course. Funny that such a state should be considered a losing, whereas to him now it would be an undoubted gaining— but more than an addendum, more like a completion. He is beyond caring. He is situated now like something otherworldly or virtual, like his world is a dream and all the creatures in his ken are makebelieve. Like the admired lady— got the sweats thinking of her, but no, not of her but of that position fixated. He speaks for no one other than himself with no attachments, no ideologies anymore, no siblings or partner or spouse or children with their twigs and branches to keep him steady on the tree. To keep him rooted. He is an entity free-floating in the universe. The universe of what? Of what other beings sapient, sentient, seeking a source, always a source. Whither Romeo, wherefore art thou? Where have you come from and where are you going in this process of slow disintegration: the pulverising of the bones, the skeleton, the skull like a million others? There are no individuals to be found in skeletons. Is that it then? The mind with its unique hankerings that keeps one going? But where does the individual go in the great scheme of things? The admired lady, her buttocks or gluteal fold are not unique, and the desire considered individual is universal in maintaining the human world's functionality, the impulse, the spur to increase the species, to keep us from becoming extinct.

A passing glance from this lady catches his eye, an awkward moment on his part being caught off guard like that from his customary coyness. But coming from her, was there a hint of a smile crossing her lips? Surely yes, friendly or as one used to having herself admired. Yes, her beauty being admired acceptingly by the glint in her eye, as she recks him, she welcomes that, but then perhaps he is perceived in some sort of non-threatening manner and her defences, if defences they are, can be let down a little for this elderly snow-haired man with the light blue eyes. Yes, the eyes, his eyes have the colour of the Mediterranean Sea or so he is led to believe judging by the bathroom mirror, for who else would tell him such a thing, except for Brother Marías; yes it was he who told him that. The lady directs her attention once more towards her daughter who is giggling, clucking like a hen at some joke the skinny boy has told. The mother calls her Maribel. It is time to go. She stands in a scarlet bathrobe which a breeze lecherously rustles and lifts to reveal long tanned legs and the derrière, staid now in its non-enhancement, but still enticing nonetheless in the fleeting glimpse of its curvature.

Maribel grimaces at her mother's call but smiles again towards the boy as she draws away as if she is being pulled by an invisible rope held by the protective *mater,* and the boy gazes after her.

And so what of Paul? One who could not marry? Who never had a relationship, someone to touch and hold, to talk to and argue with and love— ah love, that word again, perhaps venerate would be the more appropriate word in the context of its dry religious connotation, extirpated of course of its original pagan, meaning: venereal Venus, *venere*. Deprivation perhaps was his problem, as a mere child with his new Marian missal leatherbound and goldleafed which his mother had bought for him, a going-away present when he left to follow Jesus and don a black blazer with a *facere et docere* crest. He believed then, as he no longer believes, in sublimation—in overcoming the body's urges for the sake of some higher good. But it soon changed, that way of thinking, based on what he witnessed inside a contained world. Such a form of living he concluded is yet another artificial construct like words and whatever the other thing was he mentioned earlier. He is becoming more forgetful of late, it is only to be expected, one is to suppose—an early sign perhaps of the dreaded senility, so we should resign ourselves, we are being told, by whom he is not sure, to our ultimate annihilation. But he believes this tendency to forgetfulness is more due to the fact that he has no one to prod him —no wife or lover or even a melancholy whore to stab his memory into action from the hippocampus, that seahorse, to beat back the encrusting canker.

He always dabbled. He was even told he was good at sketching a likeness, but it was discouraged, dismissed out of hand in the sermons, likening them perhaps to the golden calf and the adoration of craven images—moving away from the natural course of one's destiny, if there is such a thing, by painting words on the canvas of life. Lots and lots of words, verbiage for the most part printed on murdered trees, substituting perhaps for a life lived. Because something is written, does it make it more real than the tree? Can one alter reality with the stroke of a pen or the mark of a brush?

He hears a voice, the sound of the admired lady conversing with Maribel. Is there a hint of tetchiness there, a sharpness towards her daughter? It is hard to tell through the tones of the *castellano,* adding another sense to touch, the untested erogenous zone in him and which he recognises in its purity without any clipped Andalusian letters. She is from Madrid or Salamanca perhaps escaping the summer heat of the interior of the country to take to the cooler airs of the sierras or the sea, not unlike himself perhaps, affording her time too to reflect on her life, on what was: a relationship; there had to be a relationship for her to have a daughter. But maybe she is not separated or divorced at all? Maybe her husband is merely at work and could not join her. Maybe Paul is jumping the gun here engaging in wishful thinking.

The bright Spanish light is welcoming his morning. He is sitting on his balcony looking down on the street, a busy thoroughfare with the sea distant in its simmering glaucous sheen, when he catches sight of her. The wooden gate of her villa opens and she appears dressed in a white pencil skirt of thin enough Terylene fabric to delineate her curvatures, and high heels adding to her tallness, giving her a stately bearing. She is wearing a navy blouse and her hair so shiny and dark is held back with a crystal clip that catches a glint from the sun. The presumed daughter in white shorts and widebrimmed straw hat is wired to sound and bobs along beside her strutting down the bustling street past the touts and tourist shops. The hypnotic sway of the admired lady's hips beckons him to follow.

She is sitting opposite a middleaged man in a ponytail. They are in an open air restaurant called *La Cuchara*. She is sipping coffee and laughing at some great joke. As the man reaches to touch her arm, a skinny fellow with drainpipe jeaned legs and concealed under a crash helmet suddenly appears on a motorcycle. There is a sound of several clicks from his zooming camera. She turns as he revs and speeds away.

***

Saturday comes round, so he goes to the *librería* beside *La Cuchara* at the end of his street to buy a newspaper with the weekend supplements. He likes to read book reviews, although some of his favourite books have been discovered serendipitously, and he thinks of many a fine book born like a beautiful flower to waste its sweetness on the proverbial desert air; and like some humans too perhaps living and dying anonymously quietly without a fuss, only those of note like kings worthy of a biography, and so it was but not anymore. Now it appears to be the very often talentless, loud-mouthed celebrity receiving all the attention. A cult, an elite, a clique if you wish will always dictate to us what to read and what to think. He is musing like this to himself over a *café con leche* in *La Cuchara* as he peruses the columns. After several years with the Brotherhood in South America he is quite fluent in Spanish now and, despite its different intonations, at least linguistically, his years there were not wasted.

His eye is caught by the front cover of one of the newspapers. It shows a photo of the admired lady with the heading: Minister's wife spotted on the Costa. The screen actress Viviana del Alonso, wife of the minister of the Environment Javier Moreno Alonso, caught '*coqueteando*' with film producer Benito Fudoli.

Notwithstanding the oppressive heat, the following Monday morning he travels by train to Seville to see the city of his favourite painter Diego Velázquez, remembering in particular *The Temptation of Saint Thomas*, a picture that Brother Marías had in his book of religious paintings.

He visits several bookshops and climbs the Giralda, the tallest building of the ancient world with it panoramic views of the historical city bathed now in yellow light. In a *galería* near the Hospital of the Five Holy Wounds he is equally shocked and in awe of a painting in a grey room of Helios *adulterium in dijs punitum,* surprising with his beam, Venus and Mars in *concupiscent delicto*.

In an art shop off a *bocacalle* he excitedly procures brushes and pastels and canvases and sketch pads and an assortment of charcoal and H and B sketching pencils. He even purchases a white cotton bag to put them in and a fold-up easel which he can transport on the train to kickstart his unrealised ambition.

He alights from the train back at the Costa to a commotion on the platform with people running about and shouting, some in a state of panic. He can smell burning. From the road he witnesses forest fires spreading on the nearby hills, fuelled by the drought and fanned by strong winds blowing in from the coast. The flames rage into thick plumes of smoke, desert sands and ash and pine with their cones like flame-throwers mingling and eucalyptus with their flammable resin. He sees a dishevelled man, standing confused. A couple of old village houses with rotten joists take to the caressing flames like long lost lovers. The owners of villas use blankets to extinguish smoking embers, and bits of burning wood blow in to private properties. Sunburnt tourists rush to get indoors with scarves and masks around their mouths, and others stare in anguish from their balconies at the enveloping smoke and the flames like a distant sun mocking in the hills.

Paul hears the voice of Viviana de Alonso outside the gate of her villa conversing animatedly with a guardía civil. She points in the direction of the forest. *'Mi hija, por allá.'* Her daughter gone in that direction.

Speedily dislodging his purchases in his apartment, Paul goes towards the hills. He has no fear of fire, not anymore, that threat of burning in hell is something he is well used to, fending off the advancing conflagration, renouncing damnation, all those hellfire sermons trying to bring one down down down, sinking but not anymore. God made man. No, but now he knows it was man who made god.

He catches, coming from a shop radio as he makes his way through the town, that dozens of houses have been destroyed and twenty-two people so far are declared dead or missing.

He enters the forest, stepping over the burning embers, the wild fire ripping through the dry wood and desiccated vegetation and scrubland like tinder, felling venerable oaks and cedars and fir and pine and larch, feeding its hunger with a roar. Deeper into the forest he goes, some of the trees so bent they carry the shape of the fanning wind, and he hears the screeching birds: parakeets, pheasants, startled starlings and laughing doves no longer laughing, and owls and golden eagles and nightingales all escaping in hysterical flight. Deeper and deeper he goes, fearlessly, not quite knowing what is driving him, a desire to save a life, or something else, something less tangible. And he knows it is desire for her, the mother of the girl, that propels him.

He continues to search, with a handkerchief tied around h. face and fighting back resistant branches until he sees them, the girl and the boy, under a eucalyptus tree.

They are lying on a pale brown rug of rough wool like the fisherman's rugs Paul had seen on the fishing boats. He shouts a warning, but there is no response. The boy's Olympic locks are singed and, as Paul approaches, there is no movement and the boy seems to be sleeping while shielding his beloved lying pliantly underneath him.

Paul lifts the boy, his weight unresisting (is he dead?) and, pulling up the youth's shorts to cover his modesty, places the inert body to the side on the least smouldering part of the forest floor without further investigation as Paul's urgency is to concentrate on the girl. And as he comes to Maribel a burning branch falls on her face and she, as if awakened from a dream, screams and becomes hysterical. He removes the branch and manages to lift her up before she passes out from the smoke. He carries her to safety, outdistancing the flames as they advance, and sensing a strength in himself despite his years. He deposits her gently in a clearing where firefighters intervene and ambulance alarms sound, and she is taken to the hospital in the town of U— some five kilometres away.

***

Viviana de Alonso is sitting outside the hospital ward on a grey plastic chair, maintaining a dignified if solemn demeanour. A small, stocky man is ensconced on a chair beside her. His pate is almost bald except for the tonsured greying strands and incongruously bushy sideburns. His arm is around her shoulders rubbing her back gently up and down and whispering some words too far away for Paul to decipher. But she shrugs him off. He rises and tries to pull Viviana away from her chair. '*Vamos a comer algo. Tenemos que hablar.*' Paul can hear the words now *let us go to eat, we have to talk,* but she throws him a withering glare. The man retreats, moving from her with a limp in his left foot. Paul can hear him at the end of the corridor talking rapidly in Spanish on his mobile phone.

A firefighter passes by, his face blackened by smoke—more victims have been brought into the hospital. He sees Paul in the corridor advancing towards the ward. 'Ah, you are the man who saved the girl,' he announces in a loud voice for anyone to hear. 'The way you carried her with branches burning and crashing down around you. You showed no fear. I have never seen such fortitude. You are truly a remarkable man. A hero, señor, nothing less. Please allow me the honour of shaking your hand.'

Paul thanks the officer for his kind words and approaches the ward.

'This caballero,' exclaims the firefighter, arriving on the heels of Paul and addressing Viviana, 'risked his—'

'I know,' Viviana snaps cutting him off, 'I already heard you.' She shoots a glance at Paul, incredulous perhaps that one so old could be a hero. What image does he present to her? A superman with a shock of white hair. There is a moment of mutual recognition, a slight 'Ah' from her opening lips.

'What is your name?' she asks in English.

'Paul,' he says, not feeling any need to give a surname.

'Pablo,' she says.

And an emotive chord is struck in him for he remembers long ago someone dear to him used to call him that too by the Spanish version of his name.

'Did I say something wrong?' she says noticing him reddening.

'No, not at all,' he says.

'I suppose I should thank you.'

That word *suppose,* he wonders. Why did she merely suppose?

'I was glad I could be of—'

'And you are not a...young man,' she interrupts. 'So valiant.'

'It was a terrible ordeal for you.'

'You think it was an ordeal for me?' She smiles.

'Well yes, your daughter of course,' he says in a puzzled tone.

'Of course,' she says unconvincingly, almost like a question.

'I hope she makes a complete recovery.'

'Thank you.'

'And the boy.'

'Yes, the boy.'

'How tragic.'

She does not respond but looks dreamily away down the dim corridor.

'You are Viviana de Alonso,' he continues. 'I saw your name in the newspaper. That photo.'

'Ah.' She sighs. 'I am common property it seems.'

'You speak English very well.' Oh, why did he say that? It sounds so patronising.

'Why wouldn't I, when I studied at Cambridge?' she says returning her face to regard him. 'But you are not English, the inflection.'

'I'm Irish.'

'Ah, *los nobles irlandeses,*' she says. He is confused by this lady so apparently cold and clinical after what had happened. But before they can make any further exchanges the small man returns limping hurriedly along the corridor.

'This is the man who saved your daughter,' she says.

'Ah *sí,*' he says looking directly at Paul with an attempted smile in his dark eyes. 'I have to thank you, señor, from the bottom of my heart. I am Javier del Alonso and if there is anything I can do to repay you, please don't hesitate to ask me. To ask us,' he adds nodding towards Viviana, who rebuffs the nod by turning her face away.

'Thank you,' Paul says. 'I only regret I was not able to save the boy.'

'Ah yes the boy, it was sad. *Adolescentes*, you understand. But you did all you could. Please take my card,' he says handing Paul a gold-lettered identity card. 'If you ever need anything while you are in Spain... I take it you are on a holiday.'

'Well,' Paul says. 'I came here really to paint.'

'Ah,' he says. 'How interesting, and what subjects do you paint?'

'Well so far I have sketched those old dust roads as you leave the town. I have drawn vines and olive groves and the girasol.'

'Ah yes the girasol, turning its head always to face the sun.'

'Yes with red poppies burning and cypress trees offering shade to emaciated looking horses and the colour, so much colour, bougainvillea climbing old walls of centuries old farmhouses.'

Javier rubs his leg as if to straighten a crease in his trousers. 'Yes that is our country, at least one aspect of it.' His mobile phone rings. 'Oh I am so sorry, but for now you must excuse me— an urgent call from the prime minister. I have to return to Madrid, for an important meeting.'

'About the fires?'

'Yes. Those fires unfortunately are costing the state lives and money every year. A lot of it is down to personal carelessness. I fear they may be declared a national emergency. But I will return as soon as I can, for I am concerned for Maribel's sight.'

'Ha.' Viviana scoffs. 'What do you think, señor,' she says addressing Paul, 'of a man who puts politics above the welfare of his daughter?'

Javier considers her for a moment imploringly almost with a look of helplessness, or is it despair? Paul wonders. 'You know that is not true, dear.'

'You and your meetings,' she says. 'You'd leave your daughter,' she adds challenging him and disregarding any decorum in Paul's presence, 'and expect me to stay around and look after her.'

Again Javier wavers as if he is about to say something and thinks twice about it. He turns and opens the door to Maribel's ward. There are some mutterings with a nurse. He returns and announces Maribel is sleeping soundly. 'I have been reassured by the nurse,' he says. 'Tell Maribel I will travel down to see her as soon as I can.'

'You tell her,' she says. 'She has third degree burns.'

'You think I am not aware of that?' he says. There is a moment of stony silence between them. 'Well...' he says eventually, 'I will phone later,' and then addressing Paul, 'Goodnight señor, and thank you again.'

She looks after him waddling with the imbalance in his left foot which, in another person would perhaps invoke pity, but all that is shown on his wife's face is scorn. She keeps staring after him as he goes swatting at a persistent fly buzzing around his head. And then she sighs (a sigh of relief?) as he disappears and the corridor becomes just a space.

'Are you going to stay here the whole night?' Paul says. 'You should get some rest.'

'It wouldn't be my first time to spend a night in a hospital,' she says. 'But you señor, I am obligated to repay.'

'You owe me nothing,' he says. And again a word like *obligated.* Does she not feel anything spontaneously about her daughter?

She rises from her chair. 'Excuse me,' she says. She opens the door and enters Maribel's ward. He waits politely outside wondering if he should simply go away now. And yet his virtuous act in the forest has made Viviana, even if grudgingly, beholden to him. And despite her brusque manner to her husband, it does nothing to diminish that desire in him as he surreptitiously observes the shape of her through the tight skirt. All married couples have their little tiffs, he presumes, not that he is any expert on the matter. Their next encounter could be all love and roses. But here could be opportunities for Paul as artist, were he so audacious as to articulate to this lady what he really wants in payment: to see her body in its full beautiful dénouement, to capture the curves of her flanks and the swell of her breasts. In a word, to ask her to pose for him. But how can he be so importunate to entertain such a thought of a married woman?

'She is sleeping,' she says returning. 'For now. What will it be like when she wakens, when she realises...'

'Realises?'

'That talk about her eyes. There is no reassurance from the doctor. That creature you witnessed who claims to be a husband of mine was speaking through his hat. They simply don't know. It's a matter of wait and—'

'It could be just something temporary, from the shock maybe,' he says trying to muster a caring look but unsure of the appropriateness of his words.

'Anyway,' she gestures towards her handbag, 'can I give you money? A token of—?'

'I told you already you owe me nothing.'

'There must be something I can offer you. To get done with it.'

He is conscious of the impatience in her words. *To get done with it.* She wants to dismiss him quickly, get him out of her hair, out of her life, and offering to pay him for something like that. As he fumbles to respond, she begins to regard him with less impatience now it seems to Paul. Her eyes quizzically size him up and down like a slow moving camera.

'So you are a painter, man of the snow white beard?'

'Yes.' He surprises himself by his quick self-assurance.

'Do you do paint humans, or is it just old horses and dusty roads?'

'Well yes, that is what I would—'

'Would you like to paint me?'

He blushes, recalling the old coyness.

'What is it? Don't you find me attractive?'

'Of course I do. Yes, it would give me great pleasure to paint you, madam.'

'Of course it would, and *madam.*' She laughs. 'It's agreed then. And that way all scores will be settled.'

Scores. What does she mean by that? 'I would like to sketch you first,' he hears himself saying, 'if you were to consent.'

'I do consent. Don't you know the egos of film stars?'

'I'm afraid I never got to see many films. They were frowned on in the seminary.'

'The seminary?'

'Yes, I am a former Christian Brother.'

'Ah, you poor boy, what you have missed.'

Calling him a boy at his age, he feels flattered. 'Yes, well if I do the sketch, then perhaps I could develop it into something.'

'Like a relationship?'

How quick she is. How sharp. 'Well, perhaps in a manner of speaking.'

'In a manner of speaking.' She laughs again, mocking him now.

'What I would like to do ultimately, if you were to be so kind to grant it, is a full-blown—'

'Full-blown?'

'Yes, a full-blown painting. I think you are very beautiful and I would like to—'

'Ah,' she says.

'Up to this,' he says, 'as you may have gathered, I've only done small work.'

'Small work?'

'Occasionally commissioned, of birds and trees for an illustrated nature book. But no portraits. No full portraits I mean,' for he remembers the few faces of reverend Brothers and saints from Brother Marías' book he had previously sketched. 'And sometimes of things I feared,' he adds.

'Like?'

He ponders for a moment before saying, 'Wreaths.'

'Wreaths?'

'That was later something I saw,' he says thinking of the canal, 'destroyed by water. I don't know what destroyed it.'

'How vague,' she says.

'Maybe my sketching of it was an attempt to find the cause, the origin of something.'

'And what do you think you'll find by painting me?'

'The essence of woman, perhaps. Sorry, that sounds a bit...'

'And you think you will be able to do that merely with a paint brush?'

'I don't know. I can try. If you were to allow me, that is.'

'My father dabbled,' she says looking towards the ward as if expecting the door to open.

'He was a painter?'

'Not really, he was self-educated, a constant reader, more a renaissance man, a polymath, a culture vulture who poked his nose into all the arts.' She hesitates and her eyes seem to retreat inwards into the well of memory. 'And other things.'

'Other things?'

'That old world my father followed was one in which people said "passion" rather than "lust" and thought of women as idealized goddesses.'

'Which is where I come in.'

'You see women that way?'

'I'm not quite sure. Perhaps.'

'Perhaps. Ha. My father was obsessed with education. He saved every penny to educate me. He even sent me to Italy to study art after Cambridge.'

'That is impressive,' he says not sure how best to respond to what is a boast or a simple statement of fact.

'Well, I went, he paid.'

'I see.'

'But there are things one can lose as well as gain in a university. Shall I tell you what I lost in Cambridge?'

'If you wish.'

'Yes, on the river Cam punting between Bishop's Mill and Jesus Lock, I lost my virginity there to a golden-curled fop.'

***

The rain becomes the song emanating from the tourist shop: *I've seen fire and I've seen rain* (too late to save lives). He watches the tourists with their surgical masks: fathers, mothers, lovers, children trying to ward off the pollution from the burnt earth as if it is a pestilence or evil visited upon them from outer space. The smell pungent, the fumes penetrating all the pores of the body, the nostrils, the ears, the eyes streaming, and seeping under door crevices, through the lungs, asthmatics succumbing, paramedics carrying oxygen tanks.

'Who started the fire? Was it deliberate?' a wizened woman in a shawl asks.

'The slightest thing could have started it,' the old capped man beside her replies. 'He smoked marijuana, that boy, you know, furtively, unknown to his parents.'

'So that would mean accidental.'

'Why do you stare at me? Am I to blame?'

'Of course not. The conditions were perfect for fire, wind strong, humidity low.'

'The name of the wind?'

'The desert wind, the sirocco from the Sahara whipping up the sands into a frenzy.'

'Strong enough to light the tinder to spark the impending inferno.'

'The wind blows out to the coast.'

'The *alcalde* is convinced it was started by a cigarette, caught on the video of someone's jilting mobile phone.'

'The cigarette.'

'Not the cigarette. A silver lighter was found.'

'A lighter?'

'With the initial V.'

Paul returns to the hills, his cotton bag slung over his shoulder. He is trying to recapture what had happened, that it was something real that had established itself inside his head and not some chimera. Walking through the burnt forest with its scorched branches crippled and gnarled waiting, he feels, to entangle one. He finds a rock to sit on and, taking out his sketch pad and pencils, starts to draw.

2

'Oh yes, my father, although he was only a humble town clerk, had great plans for me, and Italy was another of his ambitions like a finishing school for his daughter.'

'He wanted you to be a renaissance lady.'

She delays to throw a glance at a nurse coming out with a covered bedpan from Maribel's ward. 'She is all right?' 'Sleeping now.' Turning again to Paul, she says, 'He used to bring me to art galleries actually when I was small. We'd board a train to Madrid or Barcelona. 'He thought of me as a budding artist but never as a supine model. If he foresaw that I would do such a thing he would have been very disappointed. Those models, in their nudity were fine for others to behold, but were not for his daughter to aspire to. Oh no.' She is silent for a moment to take a breath. 'Don't you think there was an underlying hypocrisy in those cultured men?'

'You mean your father.'

'Yes, my father and his generation. But they didn't see things that way, not in those days.'

'Did you not like your father?'

'Would you like anybody who tried to suffocate you?'

And he thinks how the cloister had tried to suffocate him too.

'I would look at the paintings,' she continues, 'and think of the artists and imagine how I would emulate them. But I had not the talent really.'

'No?'

'No painterly talent or sketching ability.'

'You tried?'

'Of course I tried,' she snaps. 'But my father was blind to this. And then I got into films to his eternal regret. My first appearance was in a spaghetti western made in the arid landscape of Almería. Could you believe it? Almería pretending to be Hollywood?'

And Paul thinks Almería was probably a more beautiful place than Hollywood in a strictly geographical context, but he guesses it was the name she was after, the myth.

'I can bring you samples of my work,' he says.

'Samples remind me of a doctor's infirmary.'

'Maybe this is all remiss of me,' Paul says, 'too high a request, too intrusive into your intimacy. I would understand if your husband would not approve.'

She sighs. 'Him. Don't worry about him.'

'There are other things. The photo in the newspaper.'

'Ah yes, that was when I was with Benito and of course those provincial newspapers make a big deal of it. They have so little to gossip about. They said I was flirting, *coqueteando,* you know the word?'

'Yes.'

'When we were just talking business. He wants me to move to Italy to film, to make me into a great star and not the petty provincial that I am here. He saw my talent from an early stage. He was always encouraging towards me. Even when my husband had the accident he wanted me to continue. I think he fell in love with me, like you Pablo.'

'You think I am in love with you?'

'You are in lust with me señor, like many men. Don't think I have not noticed how you look at me.'

'Well...' he says taken aback by her forthrightness but unable to deny her truth. 'And your husband's limp, was that after...?' he says trying to steer the conversation to a more even keel.

'Let him tell you,' she says. 'I got away from him of course when I studied abroad but he always wrote or phoned telling me about his ambitions and his political rise. I thought if I went to America I would eventually break away from him, but childhood links are strong, Pablo. He kept telling me about things back home and how he missed me. Even when we were school children he kept wooing me, even then yes, bribing the chaperones with sweet things to allow him to have a private word with me, and they would turn their backs and stand behind a tree or watch demurely as my future husband stuttered and stammered into the permanence of my life.'

'But you agreed to marry him.'

'Yes, I married him.' She draws on her electronic cigarette. 'I am vaping now,' she says changing the subject, 'trying to get off the others. Not always working I'm afraid. Depends on the moment. On the mood you know.'

'I would say it is difficult.'

'You never smoked?

'No, I—'

'Anyway,' she says cutting across him, 'you asked how I could repay you and you will not take money, but you saved Maribel's life and you are an artist and you want to catch my image for the world to see, my image which is up there on the *pantalla* already. I cannot believe you must be the only man who has not seen me.

'Sorry,' he says. 'I—'

'I was on big billboards everywhere, even reclining in my vamp slit-up-the-side dress in an advertisement I remember draped across a double decker bus in London's Piccadilly Circus.' She hesitates. 'That was before—'

'Before you married him.'

'Before things changed.'

'What changed? Sorry I shouldn't...'

'It's all right,' she says, 'all the milk of human sympathy is drained of that incident now.'

'What exactly...?'

'The train crash two years after Maribel was born. Travelling to Madrid for a Cortes session when the train got derailed. His leg got crushed under the steel when he was thrown. He has a screw in his leg that he screws off every night like a wine bottle. How sexy is that, Pablo, eh? Having to look at that corkscrew every night. Try to imagine the sound of metal instead of a pumping heart.'

'It was a terrible tragedy.'

'No señor, that was not the tragedy. The tragedy was he survived.'

She rises from her chair and touches her lips with a fingernail as if remembering something and then sits down again. ' Sorry señor, I hardly know you and I am telling you these personal things.'

'That's okay,' he says, 'but why? Were you not moved by...?'

'Moved ha. I was left with a cripple, a repulsive cripple and I just on the cusp of a great career. Can you think of that? Can you think of that as fate?' She draws on her vape. 'All the hospitals, the operations, the scans, the mangled leg, and now it is all to begin again with Maribel. She does not want to meet you, by the way, and to tell you the truth I don't think I want to go through a second act.'

Blowing out the tautness around her eyes with the smoke she straightens, affording the hint of a smile.

'But enough of that. And look at you,' she says taking him in, 'with your Lawrence of Arabia eyes. With all that life saved up hiding away in the desert.'

'You could say that.'

She regards him. 'I could say anything to you, couldn't I?'

He does not answer but feels himself reddening.

'Is that a blush I see?' she says. 'You are not really an old man, are you, Pablo? You are just a lost adolescent.'

'Well,' he says, 'I thank you for your flattery.'

'It's not flattery, it's biology. We are our biological selves and not our chronological selves, are we not?'

'Oh yes.' His eyes brighten. 'That's exactly how I feel.'

Despite her hauteur, how fortunate he is to have met this woman, not only for the desire she excites in him physically, but now for her intellectual insights which she expresses so freely.

'There, you see, even though I disappointed my father I did have something.'

'Of course,' he says.

'If I didn't become a painter he wanted me to be an academic, at the very least.'

'But not the acting.'

'No more than the one-legged fellow. They were two of a kind in what they perceived as their shared ownership of me. They had the medieval view of an actress as synonymous with a harlot.'

'I'm afraid I...'

'I know, you don't feel competent to comment, and perhaps feel uncomfortable by my saying that, but they were only small roles at first like the seductress part already mentioned. Posing in that recline on a chaise longue with tight skirt and revealing thighs. Pull up your skirt higher, higher they would repeat, these directors, you know the sort of thing, to appear voluptuous a la Hollywood. It was just a game, but my father or Javier did not see it that way.' She looks straight into his eyes. 'Is that what you're after, señor?'

'You mean in my painting?'

'Whatever.'

'The image I want to create,' he says, 'is not celluloid but more interpretative.'

'Ah.'

'And subjectivised. Trying to get inside—'

'*Get inside*. You don't waste time, old man.'

'Old man. I've suddenly grown up, have I?'

'Ah, have I offended you? But everything is growing old, is it not? You think you are old. Everything is old and weary. That olive tree in the grove out there under the light of the moon is a thousand years old, look at it, the solid trunk of it, its venerable nobility. Something which you have Pablo, why I like *los olivos*.'

'I don't just mean your body that I want to...'

'Don't say, don't say my soul, please.'

'Why not?'

'There is no such a thing as a soul.'

'You think not?'

'No, not if we are evolving creatures.'

'Well, essence is perhaps the word I should use. I am trying to say not just your flesh and bones but some ethereal quality to unfathom what is in the female that induces desire in the male. I mean the quality, whatever you like to call it, that entices or invokes male biological reaction. That is what I am after.'

'If what you are saying is what makes a guy horny, you can go to pornography for that surely.'

Pornography is not art, he is about to say, but he baulks. Who is he to put his judgements on others? 'The painting,' he continues, 'would be like a learning curve.'

'For what?'

'The work. It would educate me. I have no experience of women or sex for that matter.'

'At your age? A man in your what, sixties?'

Seventy actually, he is going to say but decides not to. Let her think he is younger than what he is.

'Yes,' he says.

'You don't look that,' she says scrutinising him. 'You know, you could've been a Hollywood star.'

'I don't think so.'

'You still have good looks, *señor irlandés*. Your skin,' she says reaching over to stroke his face, 'is so smooth. The part I can touch at least, that you will allow me to touch or is not hidden by your snowy beard.' And she continues to caress him down the side of his face with her long slender fingers, inducing the redness in him again, 'Not weather or age beaten. Like my father,' she says,

'Your father?'

'Yes, so distinguished. His hair went prematurely white you know. That is what I wanted to say, you are like him in that respect, distinguished-looking, Pablo, *un hidalgo*.'

'Thank you,' he says

'Where were you hiding, like Rip van Winkle?'

'I told you I was with a religious congregation for many years.'

'So now you emerge from that chrysalis of indoctrination as a butterfly with a wounded wing. A diaphanous wing. I can see through you, Pablo.'

'And what do you see?'

'An unfulfilled man, declining perhaps.'

'Perhaps a decline before a growth or development.'

'The irony. As for me I would love the opposite to you,'

'Opposite?'

'Yes, I would like to return to that chrysalis. Can you imagine it, Paul, being in a chrysalis safe from the plotters?'

'Plotters?'

She laughs. 'How ironic the world is and now you, old virgin, want payment by way of sex education. You want me to teach you about the essence of desire.'

Again the blush. He can feel it burning, embarrassing.

'If I am not being too forthright.'

'Haven't you left it a little late?'

'I suppose I have.'

'*Suppose* ha. Anyway I left my world of makebelieve and you left your order, perhaps a place of makebelieve too, but unlike me.'

'Unlike you?'

'I take it you left on your own free will?'

'Yes.'

'Whereas I was coerced.'

'Coerced?'

'Only for my husband, I could've—'

'I am sorry,' he says, 'but surely there were compensations.'

'What compensations?'

'Maribel,' he says, 'your daughter.'

'You think that was compensation?'

'Were you not glad to have a child?'

'You know wild women have suckled wolves. You think I should have suckled a child born from his little frizzled prick?'

He doesn't know what further to say, unaccustomed as he is to such vulgarity or forthrightness, maybe that's what it is. Eventually he says, 'Why do you stay with your husband if you feel that way about him?'

'You like asking questions, old celibate,' she says.

'Sorry I...'

'Your religion, is it made up of apologies?'

Apologists, he thinks of the word.

'I belonged to it once, you know. My mother was religious.'

'Which means?'

'She was like you, Pablo.'

'Not like me anymore.'

'No, but then my father despite being oppressive, turned me away from all that grovelling. *Postrarse*. That was a word he used a lot. It was something I admired him for.'

'But you grovelled perhaps in other ways.'

'You mean the director's couch.'

'Perhaps.'

She sighs. 'No pious superiority please.'

'Sorry I didn't mean—'

She raises her hand. 'Enough,' she says rising. 'You will forgive me. I must go in and check on that silly adolescent.'

3

'Where am I?' Maribel shouts feeling the covering on her eyes.

Paul is sitting on a tubular chair which he had brought in from the corridor and which Viviana refuses, preferring to ensconce herself on the side of the bed as she tries to comfort her daughter. She had invited Paul into the ward as the 'saviour'. It seems to Paul she is calmly going through the motions, whispering to her, but with no empathy in her eyes, trying to tame her as if she were a wild cat with soft Spanish words, '*Tranquila, chica.*'

Chica, yes the cold term, not *cariña* or *hija* even. Maribel attempts to get up, but her arm tubes and her mother's arms constrain her. 'Where is Angelo? Tell me.' She reaches out for her mother but Viviana says nothing. This is not the time to tell her of Angelo's fate.

'Is that you?' she says lying back on the pillow.

'Yes it is me, Maribel.'

'Where's Papá?

'He will be here.'

'And Conchita?'

Viviana tuts. 'She is back at the villa, preparing for your return.'

Maribel tears at the eye covers.

'Leave them.'

'How long will l have to wear these things?'

'They are just there for a while.'

'A while? How long is a while? We were making love. You know that, Mother, Angelo and me, under the eucalyptus tree. Does that shock you? Are you there?'

'Yes, I am here.'

'But then nothing would shock you, would it? He knew about love, not like you. His whispered words *te quiero*. On his lips which I kissed and kissed to hear the words over and over. Did your lovers say words like that to you, Mother?'

'Maribel, please.'

'And that Italian Romeo of yours with the ponytail, did he tell you that he loved you more than Papá did.'

Viviana does not answer. She looks towards Paul who casts downwards under her stare.

'Where's Angelo? Is he all right? And where's Papá?' Shrill desperation increases in her voice. 'These covers,' she says touching her eyes again, 'am I blind? Is that it? That burning branch,' and she cries out again and a nurse peeps in and then after a moment or two calmly, as if in a reverie, Maribel says, 'Oh and yes he was still and I wondered was he breathing. Yes, he had been breathing hard.'

'Were you smoking stuff?' Viviana says.

'Had to follow your example, hadn't I?'

'Too much stuff.'

'But that hard breathing was to be expected after all as we made love. Then he lingered and I nudged him but he did not move. We were so close, I had not the heart to ask him to lift himself. I wanted to stay like that with him forever. Do your lovers breathe hard, mother when they are in the throes? Angelo was breathing hard and then he was still. And there was the smell of burning and I must've fallen asleep and then someone came, yes some busybody came and hoisted my angel off me.'

'It is all right now, Maribel,' Viviana says. She reaches out her hand as if to touch her daughter but holds back.

'But is he all right?' She grips the sheet tightly, showing the white of her knuckles 'He did not die. Did he? Tell me Angelo did not die' She cries out once more as sweat begins to trickle down through the bandages on her face.

'She has a temperature,' Viviana whispers to Paul as she touches her daughter's forehead. 'Please call the nurse.'

He goes to the corridor and summons a portly nurse pushing a trolley from a ward. Rattling away in fast dialect she administers an injection to Maribel whom she finds difficult to contain, as the girl kicks the bedclothes and twists and turns calling out for Angelo. Eventually her voice grows weaker and she succumbs to sleep.

'Pray for her,' Viviana says.

'You say pray for her and yet you don't believe.'

'You are the Brother, the reverend, the miracle maker.'

He stirs uneasily, recognising the mockery in her voice but says nothing.

After a final cursory glance at her daughter, Viviana rises. 'She will sleep now.'

At the door she turns and says, 'You may bring some of your work tomorrow if you wish. In the morning,' she adds, 'but not too early.'

***

The sun beckons from the window waking him, with its orb early rising making him feel uncomfortable, summoning him from his bed, more effective than any alarm clock, causing him to feel remorseful as he once felt over missing prayers, guilt-induced to lie there in such bright light. For fear like in Irish weather it could melt away.

He thinks of Viviana as he showers and her ambivalent attitude towards her daughter. But the overriding obsession, the desire for her body, and her beauty, is nullifying all book-learned morality, apprehending him like a chain tightening. And Maribel, that unfortunate girl, he berates himself for not feeling strongly enough for her welfare. She is not simply a pawn in a fractious marriage. She a victim. But he did save her. Should he have done that considering how she had referred to him as a mere busybody? Oh no, the thought is against all of what he did believe. But look at the state of her now. She is clearly disturbed and does not mean what she says.

He announces himself at the intercom and the wooden gate opens.

'You came.'

'Yes.'

She is sitting in a bathrobe on a sunbed by the heart-shaped pool.

'Sit down,' she says.

He sits on a wicker chair near her, resting his cotton painting bag with the long handles at his feet.

'Do you like the pool?'

'Yes, the shape of it.'

'A heart, just like they have in Hollywood.

A small middle-aged woman with greying hair comes through the French doors carrying a tray of glasses and iced water.

'Leave us,' Viviana snaps at the maid as soon as she has placed the tray on the low table by Viviana's sunbed.

And then to Paul, smiling, 'I wasn't sure you would come. I thought I might've frightened you away.'

'No,' Paul says smarting at Viviana's rough treatment of the maid (the goddess showing her mortal side) who head-bowed is retreating now back through the French doors.

'You know,' she says sizing him up, 'if I were to say what Don Quijote were like in the flesh, you would fit the picture. You are as thin as him, as angular and as...

'Old, were you going to say old?'

'No, but saving damsels in distress like you saving Maribel.'

'I am very fond of Don Quijote.'

'And why would that be?'

'He had an innocence I suppose, a naivety.'

'Could you save me, Don Pablo?'

'Save you from what precisely? I mean are you in danger?'

She regards him from under hooded eyes. 'Are you really innocent, Paul?'

'Well...' He doesn't quite know what to reply.

She takes a cigarette from a packet and rooting in her handbag says, 'I'm still missing that damned lighter.'

'Oh,' Paul says, feigning ignorance but thinking of the villagers' comments and wondering why she is not vaping.

'It was the boy, he had no *fuego*.'

'You gave him the lighter?'

'Not I. He was smoking weed, the indica form which induces sleepiness.'

'How do you know?'

'I found some in Maribel's shoulder bag.'

'And how do you know it induces sleepiness?'

She stares at him. 'How do you think I know?'

'Sorry, I...'

She locates a box of matches in her handbag and lights her cigarette. Curling the smoke towards Paul she says, 'Enough about them now, señor Picasso. As regards my posing, which way do you want me?'

'Well...'

'Out with it, *guapo*,'

He thinks of the first time he saw her diving in the water, how arousing it was, but he has not the courage, not yet at least to ask her to pose in such a manner, so he says, 'Perhaps we could start with the face.'

'Oh *Viejo,* is that all you want?'

'If that is not importuning you too much.'

'Importuning ha. I pose for you but you are the one who feels uncomfortable. The words you use, señor. But first,' she says moving a hand to her back, 'will you draw me this way?'

'Which way?'

'Scratching,' she says erupting into a raucous laugh.

'Yes, the boy smoked,' she continues nonchalantly as Paul takes out his sketch book and some pencils from his cotton bag.

'And Maribel,' he says starting to draw, holding his pencil vertically between forefinger and thumb, gleaning her dimensions from head to shoulder, 'you allowed her to smoke joints?'

'I didn't allow her or I didn't disallow her,' she says suddenly irritable.

'What does that mean?' he says stalling his pencil.

'It means you are asking too many questions. You are becoming tiresome, Pablo, showing your age, your moral stance.'

'No.'

'No?'

'Not that please,' and he wonders is he to be shackled with that word *moral* for ever?

'Anyway,' she continues, 'the boy, her little angel as she calls him, was to call to the villa before the night of the fire to bring her on a date. And she pranced about in her new Cuisa mini dress excitedly waiting for him. But he did not turn up.'

'No?'

'It appears his uncle Antonio, his mother's brother, had insisted that he accompany him on the fishing boat that day for a big haul.' She pulls on her cigarette. 'But the following night, the night of the fire, he did come to the villa.'

'You met him?'

'No. I pretended I had to go somewhere, that I had something planned that night. But I knew by Maribel's frequent mirror consultations in her new jeans—she had binned the mini dress in a rage—I knew that something was afoot.'

'So you...?'

'So instead of going out I banged the front door and hid in the adjoining room. I was fearful, curious what my stubborn daughter was up to. After a while I heard her greeting the boy, and he was so contrite for missing their first date, and he enquired if I was around. "Don't worry about her," my darling daughter said and then added with her customary venom, "She's probably gone to meet one of her lovers."'

Paul freezes.

'And then.' Viviana continues, 'I heard her asking the boy why he was holding an unlit cigarette. "I have no matches," he said. "Here, take this," she said and I could see through the crack in the door Maribel handing over my silver lighter which she had found under some magazines.'

'Your lighter?' Paul says.

'Yes,' she says, 'and now I am growing tired, Pablo.'

'Of course,' he says, 'these sketches are just preliminaries.'

She rises and looks over his shoulder at the drawings. 'The nose is crooked,' she says.

'I always have problems with noses. I can make adjustments.'

'Adjustments to the nose?'

'Well...'

'You said you had other stuff.'

'Oh yes,' and he takes out some canvasses from his cotton bag. The small watercolours and drawings he had done on the byroads of the town which he had mentioned to Javier he shows her, but also of the favelas of Brazil and locations from his youth, the pencil drawings, and saved clandestine sketches from the monastery, and some from memory, an attempted self-portrait which he was not at all happy with when he was a postulant just arriving at the doors of the monastery with his oiled coif, ironed white shirt and of course his cardboard suitcase.

'That was you.'

'Yes, starting off.'

'Starting off?'

'In my vocation.'

'I see, and this one, this tall man with the sad eyes,' she says, 'pointing to a pencil sketch of Brother Marías, 'he was a reverend brother.'

'My mentor. He was born in Spain, not far from here in fact.'

'Ah. Your pencil slipped there,' she says pointing at a facial scratch.

He remembers that occasion. It was when he was discovered by the Brother Superior. He was reluctant to hand over the drawing, and the pencil which was hovering slid over the face.

'And the impoverished barrios of San Salvador.'

'Yes.'

'Ha.'

Is it a sneer? Her crinkled-up nose says it's a sneer.

'What do you work with?'

'Normally...'

'Normally? Is there a normality in art?'

He thinks of a different word. Generally, that will do.

'When I finish with the chalks I... generally proceed with free and subtle brushwork using Walnut, lapis lazuli, red lacquer.'

'And that drawing,' she says, pointing to the charcoal sketch of a woman. 'She looks like the Madonna except her left breast is exposed. Were you trying to combine the sacred and profane, Pablo? Is that what you are trying to tell me? Is that what you are about?'

He swallows, looking down in embarrassment pretending to sort out some pencils and brushes in his cotton bag. And he remembers being transfixed in a gallery in Dublin by Bernard van Orley's *Holy Family*, something which would not have been in Brother Marías' book on religious paintings: the Mother offering her breast but the child's gaze was upwards and beyond looking for more. What more could a child desire? A mother's breast, was that not enough? Something ethereal. The young Pablo in the oversize sables willing his vocation to be sincere. And this child, what more did he know? What more did he seek?

He is fiddling, afraid to look up like a shamed schoolboy.

Eventually when he does straighten he sees her grinning at him. 'Are you up to such an undertaking, Pablo?'

'Yes,' he says trying desperately to force a resoluteness in himself.

'Have you anyone back in Ireland, relatives I mean?'

'No, both my parents are long since dead and any distant family are all gone.'

'So nobody would know if you were not to... return.'

'No, why do you ask?' he says surprised by such an ominous question.

'Just curious. Never mind,' she says. 'Let me show you something.' She takes out from her handbag which is lying by the sunbed a small pistol with a diamond stud embedded into its pearl handle.

'I want you to look at this,' she says handing it to him.

'What, a pistol? What would I want with such a thing?'

'It too is art, don't you think? More sculpture than painting I admit. Familiarise yourself with it. It's a .32 calibre, small but effective.'

'Effective?'

She hands the diminutive weapon to him. 'Examine the exquisiteness of its ornate barrel.'

'Where did you get such a thing?'

'A prop from one of my films. It was meant as an ornament, a gift from the film producer, to keep in a glass cabinet.'

'But why are you showing this to me?'

She tilts her head to regard him. 'I don't like keeping things in glass cabinets, Paul.'

Which way do you want me? Maybe she meant laughing or solemn.

What could he answer other than what he did? He had not thought of the face. How would the face respond to the gazed-at rear? A sideways glance. Yes, it had to be that, not what he wanted but, knowing her as she is now, it had to be not merely laughing but mocking.

Be yourself, he would have liked to have said, even if that was not the total truth. What he really would have like to have said was, be what I would like you to be, be the person that is in my mind, not the person that speaks so tauntingly. So which self? she would say, being the actress.

And he knows he cannot answer. She has him. She is directing, and showing him that pistol as she did. He is just a limp brush splashing paint on a canvas.

4

No one objects as he watches over Maribel in her hospital bed. Nurses smile at him in their coming and going, recognising him from the newspapers. He is the hero after all, the feted life safer. Maribel jerks and feels the tautened skin around her face. She is trying to come to terms with her stainless enamelled world. Maybe she forgets for a moment what has happened. She forgets about Angelo. Is she awake? Or immersed in a dream with some god playing a trick on her, preventing her from seeing. Blindfolded? She touches her face again, realising. 'No,' She calls for her father. He has gone, the portly nurse tells her but will be back, and Conchita, there is no Conchita. It's my mother's doing, isn't it? She won't let Conchita come.' 'But your mother—' 'No, I do not want her,' and then as if suddenly remembering she cries out. 'Oh Angelo. Bring my Angelo to me, mi Angelito, tell me he is all right. Don't say the fire touched him.'

'She does not know about the boy yet,' the nurse whispers in the corridor to Viviana. 'It is best that way until she improves.'

'You say improves. You don't believe she will fully recover?'

'Third degree is the worst form, goes through the dermis, affects deeper tissues but otherwise when there is no change of dressing she does not feel. She just lies there numb.'

'How can that be?'

'Because the nerve ends are destroyed. The epidermis and hair follicles are destroyed which means new skin will not grow. She is to be transferred to a burn centre in Málaga for debriding.'

'Debriding?'

'To remove the dead skin. She will have to get a skin graft.'

He makes his way out of the hospital and, despite the lateness of the evening, the heat is still overpowering, exacerbated by all the burning emanating from the mountain. He can't get her scream out of his head as they changed her dressing. The young girl in agony, red blistered swelling that would heal in three weeks, the surgeon said. 'Keep the wound clean and protected.' The order overheard to the flustered nurse. They are using antibiotic ointment.

A fire brigade wails past. Why is he, ex-cleric, worn-out husk, really here in Spain? If that is what he is. He questions himself as he always does umpteen times, every action and no action. Every thought is an interrogation. He chose Spain for the light, the brightness of a world illumined by a powerful sun that appears almost every day. And how dark it is now for one of its indigenes. Another of life's ironies. In Ireland the rain wears the pants and the sun is such a rare thing, a distant relative who seldom calls. He wanted to see the world lit up like the halos over the saints' heads. Was that just a fiction, an artistic illusion like so many other things? But he likes to believe that aura exists: it has merely been darkened out and is there in the bright world making clear our humanity. That is what he wants more than anything else after the dark circumscribed years of greyness in Stygian corridors smothering one's being with gloomy dread and black guilt for everything in the world. All those things we are unworthy of and which we were indoctrinated to believe. We could never make the grade. Always act as an abased creature with some glean of hope perhaps in South America where he became attracted to liberation theology. But Helios there was contained by clanking chains. What made him? What unmade him? His undoing. A part of him like a branch never allowed to bloom or produce foliage, a branch turning sickly as the year advances, browning as it prepares to die, a dead scion ready to fall off. And he is the tree now suddenly conscious of his wounded limb and needs to send sustenance to it in a last ditch effort to save it.

And he remembers, Brother Marías' Robinia needs watering.

5

The next morning he breakfasts on a cereal of corn flakes and pumpkin seeds, a natural anti-inflammatory to ease his prostate problem. He had read about their benefit in some book *How not to die*. Natural ways to survive or at least prolong the process along cemetery road.

Banishing the thought, which has a tendency to rise occasionally in his mind, of the unopened letter lying at home, he turns to the pages of the *Diario* and reads about the cinder path smouldering and the smoke and the burning of the feet and the loss of life in the young boy and some sheep and goats caught in the brambles. The boy was a native of the neighbouring village of G — which he decides to visit by taking a local bus. The bus is jammed with gossiping *señoras* and men with weather-worn faces engaging in passionate discussion with the bus driver (who looks upon the driving as a mere secondary activity) about the fires and the boy. Everyone is talking about the boy.

It is an authentic Spanish village untainted by tourism with lots of little shops and cafés with old men playing dominos and drinking black coffee from small glasses and smoking cigars. The village was founded by fishermen and has statues of two fishermen celebrating their catch in the main square. The local boy Angelo Machado who had gone to the forest with Maribel on a tryst was the son of one of those fishermen and the shops are closed now in mourning with black drapes across their doors. She had been on holiday in the area with he mother, when she met the boy Angelo Machado. Her mother, the newspaper reports, is the screen actress Viviana del Alonso, previously known as Viviana Gil Ortega, and a native of the village of G—, and now wife of the government minister Javier Moreno del Alonso. The two youths were frequently seen dallying with each other by the sea near the villa where the mother and daughter were staying. The señora was not available for comment to the press or media and requested that her privacy be respected at such a delicate time. The minister, on being contacted by the press, said his daughter was fortunate to be alive. Their actions were an example of the folly of youth, going into the woods when all the burning signs were there. Only for an elderly man who, by some miracle happened to appear at the scene and ignoring the falling and burning trees and the pallor of suffocating smoke, risked his own life to save his daughter before the ambulance men and paramedics arrived, who he must add were most vigilant in the administration of their duties. But alas, they were too late to save the boy who, overcome by the fumes and smoke inhalation and possibly from the ingestion of soporific drugs according to the medics, was dead when they got to him. The minister also expressed sympathy to the boy's family, and funeral services will take place after a postmortem has been carried out.

'You saw him?' she says.

'Yes, he greeted me briefly. I read they are trying to bring in some legislation about the fires.'

'There are always fires.'

'Are you all right?' he says seeing the scorn rising in her.

She sighs, one of her long sighs which he is now becoming familiar with. 'It's all to do with timing, isn't it? In the movies, in life? I was on the cusp.'

She strikes a match to light a cigarette.

'What happened to your ecigs?' he says.

'Not today. I am not in the humour for those electronic things.'

'And the lighter, it was found?'

'I don't want to talk about it, okay?'

'That's okay.'

'And now this happening and Maribel, they have jeopardised my chance in Italy. Blowing out smoke in a long exhalation she says, 'He sees no danger in you.'

'Who?'

'My husband.'

'He considers you innocuous.'

'Thank you.'

'He thinks you are too old to be any danger.'

'Danger?'

'My husband is a jealous man Pablo, but like me he is beholden to you. So he gives his blessing for the portrait. You wonder perhaps how we became estranged?'

'Well...'

'The parting of our ways should have happened with the possibility of me going to Hollywood and him becoming more active in politics. But there was always that childhood nonsense.'

'What do you mean?'

She sighs. 'He was fixated on me. He never stopped pursuing me with promises and flattery, and I fell for it, señor. I gave up my career for that, that specimen you witnessed.'

'I'm sorry,' he says, 'but if you had been determined perhaps...'

'Determined? I was never determined. That's my problem, isn't it?'

'So instead of going to Hollywood, you married him.'

'Yes. And in the meantime it was he who was the rising star.'

'You mean in politics.'

'Yes. Of course I have to admit in the beginning I was flattered when he became a minister and I accompanied him, our minister for the environment on many media engagements throughout the EU and smiled into press cameras and I was his charming wife on display at his side. We were in Brussels and Paris many times where he never lost an opportunity to use me to win the media over and ensure coverage of whatever he was spouting about in all the papers and of course on television and the fickle social media where the supposed good looks of a so-called feted screen actress were duly exploited.

'So what happened?'

'I got pregnant, didn't I?'

'I see.'

She ponders. 'I could've loved my daughter maybe if I'd had her later with someone else. I conceived her in a moment of stupidity.'

'We all have regrets,' he says and he knows it is the wrong unfeeling phrase, 'but Maribel... her eyes, is she still...?'

'Still the same. Perhaps she will be better off.'

'What do you mean?'

Extinguishing her cigarette in the small glass ashtray, she says, 'Who wants to see the sordidness of this world?'

6

He is standing on the beach in the half-light, a silver colour on the waves forlorn in shedding and receding once more, having spent themselves on the shore. He paints with deft, confident strokes almost hurried as precursors of what he is ultimately about, the sea, the crepuscular sky, his easel unsteady in a sudden gust. A gull squawks, a child in the distance shouts in unison steady now making captive of the lascivious Neptune. It is growing too dark to image it but he will remember it and draw from it, draw from your dream of a place like van Gogh had done. He thinks of van Gogh in the changing light, the sky vermillion but no yellow, no sunflower as yet but the cosmos always there as in the beginning, the mountain in the distance like a supine whale and the sea shiny in its foam frothing, hungry to consume the land, to mate, this coming together of sea and earth guided by the moon clandestine almost in the quiet of the twilight, a coitus, a shedding again and again since the beginning of time, and we haughty creatures making rules.

She is standing some distance away, her silk beach robe hovering like a wave revealingly blown thigh high by the cheeky wind. She calls his name like an echo in the wind soft, the soft word of PA B LO. The sea answers with its deadly chorus. PA B LO, the word so strange, he being authenticated on a foreign tongue. Who is that person being invoked? He turns around, his brush held aloft. She smiles, tilts knowingly now as she dives.

He tries to convince himself that all this is normal. That all this is quite...okay. All this going on, being sucked into the nuances of the life of a beautiful woman, of a family, of tragedy and discontent, how to get his own head around all this, and all the time he knows it is this beauty that propels him.

The following morning she sits for him by the swimming pool of the villa propped up on a sunbed. Fully clothed in her one-piece navy swimsuit and white-towelled beach robe. And he considers the swimsuit, so patrician compared to the proletarian bikini. It has its own erotic makeup nevertheless, being less one dimensional, less focused on one area; the desire is now on the totality of the whole woman.

'Start somewhere, *por dios*,' she says with a touch of exasperation in her voice, for he had been oscillating for what seemed like an age to her now between inanimate charcoal and pencil silhouettes and gesture drawings and aspects of the sea always a safe option. And yet he knows like an explorer he has to start feeling his way across the atlas of her face, his pencil leading him through unchartered territory, the forest of her brows, the mountain of her nose, the pools of her eyes, the canyon of her mouth.

'A part that's already naked,' she says.

'Already naked?'

'Like my eyebrows.' She laughs that derisive laugh again. 'Don't you think they are very bushy, a mock simile of the hair down below so they can be considered sexy or masculine in their hirsuteness depending on your point of view. I want to know, Pablo, what is your point of view.'

Her eyebrows, he is not happy with. Despite using the maulstick, his hand did shake and her eyebrows became thick and indeed hirsute, odious in their lack of femininity. And the vulgar manner in which she had referred so casually to 'down below', but he must act; he wills himself as if it is normal parlance.

'No,' he declares like a eureka moment, placing his pencil down on the low glass table she affords him. 'I know now what it means.'

'What what means?' she says.

'Remember you asked if I ever lurked inside myself? That's it.'

'What's it?'

'In the drawing. You are the conduit.'

'The conduit, ha.'

'Sorry, I hope I haven't offended you but what I mean is when if ever I have this work completed there will hopefully be harmony in my life because I intend to invest all the parts of myself into it.'

'All the parts,' she says. You are saying there is not harmony in your life, Pablo?'

'No,' he says somewhat flustered by her interrogatory tone. 'I thought I had made that clear earlier. The institution—'

'Ah, the institution. I remember.'

There is mockery in her tone once more but he continues anyway. 'It is our desires that make us.'

'You think that?'

'Yes, I realise that now. And if by making the drawing and later the painting I can harness my desire and get to the source of it, then I will have portrayed not so much you, but myself.'

'Yourself?'

'Please bear with me while I follow this thought process through,' and his brush hangs drippingly. 'What I am saying is the portrait I hope to make of you will ultimately point to me, like a mirror revealing who I am. What I mean is by completing the painting, it will have expunged...

'Expunged?'

'Whatever is inside me, whatever is incomplete in me.' He places his brush back in its palette. 'I am sorry. I don't know if that makes any sense to you.'

'Ah,' she says, 'now I get it. You mean like *The Picture of Dorian Gray* and that evil painting in the attic. I like that. I like that there is evil lurking in the ex-cleric.'

'No, I don't mean that. I don't mean evil, and besides that is relative term.'

'And what of *my* desires?' she says uncrossing her legs enticingly.

'You must tell me.'

'They are a medley.'

'A medley?'

'Women I will have you know are made of nine parts of desire. And men are only one out of the ten god created, if you are to believe the Koran.'

'You read the Koran?'

'The necessary parts.'

'Of course.'

'Women are a mass of physical attractions. I will have to teach you, old pupil. You will learn they are a cauldron of emotions.'

'Such as?'

'Feeling kind and selfless, those obnoxious terms.'

'You don't like the virtues?'

She reflects for a moment, then says, 'There are other more motivating emotions.'

'Like?'

'Oh all these questions,' she says suddenly frowning and putting her hand to her forehead. 'Enough.'

'Are you all right?'

'Call Conchita,' she says. 'I need to take my medication.'

7

He struggles with his mode of operation afterwards on the balcony of his apartment, the rent for which he is able to mange with the modest stipend left to him by his late father. Pencils or brushes, sketchpad or canvas? Those eyebrows, the face, ideas of his own makeup superimposing an image, telling more about himself than his subject, the damned ego always interfering on the pure image which he is trying to create. And besides, it wasn't only eyebrows or noses he was having trouble with but raw flesh, raw matter. And she, frowning on the virtues (the four cardinal virtues and the seven deadly sins rote-learned are drumming in his head); and the dismissing of him and calling for her medication. For what? A mere headache? Or is it underlining something more serious? He realises he simply does not know her well enough yet for her to stand alone, to stare out from canvas at him from her own occlusion and with her own autonomy.

Abandoning his sketching and painting efforts, he walks the streets leading down to the sea and in the distance the mountains and the smouldering earth and all the dispossessed hundreds of people without their homes. Where will they stay? Javier the minister is trying to rehouse them in temporary homes and stadiums, he read that in the Diario. And yet life goes on. The outdoor cafés are lit up with people drinking post-prandially, or others side-stepping shrieking youngsters heading for discos: the short skirts of the girls like lodestones leading the young men on towards the garish lights and loud music of the discos. He scrutinises the faces of older women, mature women but still in their prime, holding onto their spouses or partners, delighting in some knick-knack they have purchased in the tourist shop. Others stall to kiss lengthily or peck and saunter hand in hand as if they are immortal and commandeer time. And he notices solitary women too wandering rather forlornly embellished for some occasion that did not materialise. He observes their eyebrows painted or pencilled, few of them as bushy as Viviana's and he marvels at their beauty in the mysterious illumination of twilight and he thinks of Viviana's face. He must capture that too, to mirror, to equate with the other parts of his desire. To remove the harshness there. But would that be dishonest?

A wanderlust after all the years of following rules, of being proscribed, the saintly image one had to project, a vocation that was lost somewhere along the way. Institutional religion is second-hand where one is not being directed to the immediacy and individualisation of spiritual experience. All one got were dry old books and dark cloisters. When he resided in the monastery it was like he was in hospital with a sickness in his psyche.

Apart from the obvious celibacy vows, the spur, the real motivation to leave it all was the ideology itself. The dogmas became too narrow for him. Was God contained in the man-made chalice or in the golden Helios, free-shining, teaching our beings to glow with its light? So he sought it to see his new apotheosis in at its best its full splendour, beaming from the blue of a Mediterranean sky. Here he can wander and engage in free enquiry on his existential journey, something he never got a chance to really do, blinded as he was by the narrow dictates of an ideology. God, he now realises, is simply a point of view and, as for the immortal soul, its very existence he now begins to doubt after his discussion with Viviana (whatever else one can say about her, she is an intelligent woman). If we are supposed to be evolving creatures, as she says, if to be human is to change, where can such a thing as a soul in its unchanging essence fit into the scheme of things? And even that, even the word *schema* in all its Kantian logic, was there ever such a thing?

***

The next morning he phones the villa, having got the number from Conchita on his way out the previous day. It is Viviana who answers, surprisingly sweet-toned. She is fine, she says after his enquires. 'Who wants to talk about yesterday? Of course come over. I'll be waiting.'

On entering the gate of the villa a stocky man with a briefcase is briskly leaving. Paul stands aside to let him pass. 'Good day, señor,' the man says.

She is sitting head reclining on her sun bed by the pool of the villa, the sun exuding a companionable warmth before reaching its midday intensity. Clad in the same black bikini which she was wearing the first day he saw her, but her tan is darker now, her hair a glorious shining wave held in by the same crystal clip. She is back to her vaping.

'Are you feeling better?' he says.

'Don't cross the line,' she shouts.

There is no line anywhere. Paul pretends to examine the tiled floor where nothing is marked out but he is afraid to say it, judging by the sharpness of her tone.

'I can work from here,' he says. He is a yard or two away from her.

'Good,' she says. 'Now we can commence. You ask me how I am.'

'Yes I was just—'

'It appears I have a pulse rate that passes the limit of reason. That's what Doctor No Fuss says. It races in my brain causing these headaches. Do you ever get headaches, Pablo? I mean galloping horses in your head?'

'Not really. But you think that sometimes our minds can—'

'Pass the limit of reason?'

'Yes.'

'What do you think, Paul?'

'I don't know.'

She shrugs and sits up. 'Anyway, it is good to see you, wise old man. Once you keep your distance.'

'Okay.'

'And don't ever get rid of that shock of white hair.'

'I don't intend to.'

'There, you see,' she says holding the pulse on her wrist. 'I don't get excited when I see you.'

'Great,' he says wondering if she is conscious of her ambiguity.

When he has settled at his easel, she says, 'In my last film I had to kill my husband.'

He laughs. 'Really?'

'I had to kill my husband,' she repeats icily, 'with the aid of my lover.'

'Your lover.'

'Yes, in the film. Are you listening to me?'

He is fiddling in his artist's bag, attempting to appear nonchalant. 'Yes, I am listening.'

'Look at me.'

He looks up.

'Lovers can be older. You know that, Pablo.'

'Well...' He feels unnerved under her scrutiny. But then as the sun hits her slantingly she budges and says, 'Sorry, you were saying.'

'I wasn't really saying anything.'

'No?'

'But I am grateful to you for having said what you did about the aged I mean.' He stalls for a moment, then says, 'What I was thinking...'

'What were you thinking, Pablo?'

'Well, when you were talking about the film I was thinking how strange it is that men have the capacity to create life and yet also to end life.'

'Is it really that strange?' she says.

Conchita appears with a tray.

'Ah tea, how you English like tea.'

'I'm not English,' he says.

'Oh sorry. Have I offended you? It the same with us and the Portuguese, slips of the tongue. But you do like tea?'

'Yes, I like tea.'

'Have no fear,' she says as Conchita pours tea into small China cups, 'there will always be a woman with a shopping bag to cater for your needs.'

He does not speak. He thinks that is a quote from somewhere but can't place it. He becomes uneasy at Viviana's curt dismissal of the maid with a wave of her hand. Why does she have to treat her so coldly?

'An artist's needs,' she says pondering. 'What are they? You think you should be gifted a muse. Think again. You were hidden away, remember? Well the world has changed.'

'I know that. I know the world is always changing, but some things remain the same, fundamental, like the modes of being.'

'How grandiose, how positively patrician you sound like those Cambridge cads or pompous Salamanca students. Ha, you want to intellectualise art. You can't do that. It's all myth, Pablo, don't you know. All those paintings of men's desires purporting to be art. There is no Eve, there is no fig leaf of control. What difference other than a titillation does it make whether it is the *maja vestida* or the *maja desnuda*. Your desire is a transitory thing.'

'It is the life force I believe.'

'In the male perhaps, but there are other things.'

'Like your daughter, perhaps. Filial love.'

That stops her flow. She looks lost for a moment. He should not have said what he said. But she recovers and says sharply, 'I have to be her eyes, don't I now? I will have to lead her like a guide dog. You think that's fair?' She shouts. 'You honestly think that's fair?'

8

In the village of G— there are whispers. With his Spanish as he wanders through the markets, he is able to make out the sibilants murmured conspiratorially on the lips of the sable-dressed widows who lost their husbands at sea, *qué lástima, qué horor* for his poor madre and the poor boy who always had the heart condition, a hole in his heart, a grey-haired woman with beads intones. Yes, says the first widow, a woman with a shawl, an inborn condition, a delicate baby in his mother's womb and his father lost at sea. *Ah mi,* half his life in thrall to the great ocean, as many of the men of the village were, swept away in a storm, their little fishing boats not strong enough to withstand what the sea has to throw against them. The *pescadores* have a tough life, *ay mi.* How strange that it should be the opposite of water that should kill the young boy. Ah fate, it will decide how and when we are all to go. But it was not the fire, says the widow with the beads. The fire was only what followed. Too much excitement in the young, says the widow with the shawl, they think young love is theirs only like a new flower just bloomed. *Ay mi,* how short the bloom. I had heard of the girl, the rich spoiled daughter of the film star. *Ah mi,* the jumped-up native Ortega thinks she is too good for us. They think they have entitlement seducing a young boy leading him astray deep into the forest. The siren led him to have her way with him, the innocent boy, yes he was innocent for he was known and liked, yes liked by all of us in the village and she came here to disrupt our lives, the *sinvergüenza.* She got her comeuppance you know, says the widow with the beads. She has been struck blind. *Ah mi.* The fates will always have their revenge when they are tested. Serves her right for using the boy for her own lascivious desires. It was not the young girl's fault, says the widow with the shawl, who are we to say? And how was she to know of the congenital condition of poor Angelo? It is the mother I would blame going off making movies when she should have been minding her child. A boy at puberty with the growing testosterone like a young toro would not reveal a weakness, least of all to a girl he was trying to impress. First love, *ah mi*, says the widow with the beads. He wanted to appear strong and valiant like the *marineros* and *pescadores* of our village. Like his father and uncle.

***

'Maribel is home?'

'She is no better.'

'It is taking a long time.'

'Too long. The doctors keep saying to be patient but she is distraught. She still needs to be sedated.'

'You sedate her?'

'Of course. Regularly with morphine after the debriding. I watched the nurse.'

'Regularly, you say. Could there be a danger of addiction?'

'What do you expect me to do? I have to take her out of pain, don't I? Her skin torments her but not nearly as much as her not seeing. She screams in her sleep like she is reliving the inferno and cries out for her Angelo. She curses you.'

'I gathered that.'

'And me of course she has no time for me either, just her papá as if he were some saint.'

'Is he not busy with the fires. The aftermath?'

'Ironic isn't it, his own daughter caught up in all of this.'

And your daughter too he is about to say, but all he says is, 'It is ironic.'

'Nothing but gloom and doom ever follows in his wake.'

'You think her condition is permanent?'

'Possibly.'

'What you said last time about the sordidness of the world, about her being protected by not seeing it, you really believe that?'

'Ha, I never said that?'

Paul does not respond for a moment. Eventually deciding to overlook the lie, he says 'How will she manage I mean as she goes through life?'

'There you go with your myths again,' she says straightening herself on the wicker chair. 'Do you want to meet Maribel? She doesn't want to meet you. She hardly wants to thank you. All the others are thanking you. You are a man of valour, you realise that, Paul. Here,' she says, taking a newspaper from a stool, 'I kept this,' and she hands him the *Diario* of some days ago on the front page of which there is a photo of himself coming out of the forest carrying the girl, eyes smoke-rimmed and white beard blackened, *el héroe* and the article proceeds with an account of the valour of a *viejo*.'

'Does that make you feel good?'

'I must've missed that article,' he says, remembering only the brief mention of himself that he read of earlier.

'Ha,' she says. 'You know what Maribel thinks, what I have had to listen to for the last number of days since she came out of hospital?'

'What does she think?'

'She blames you for leaving her Angelo there to die. That's what the dim-witted villagers are saying too. They're spreading the rumour you saved the rich kid and left the poor kid to die.'

'Who told you this?' Paul asks, astonished.

'It comes from the mouth of our chief gossip here, Conchita. She lives in the same village.'

'But Conchita hardly—'

'According to her, the boy's mother is inconsolable. Señora Machado,' she says spitting out the name. 'I knew her and her sisters. Jealous people, never wished me well.'

'I could not carry both of them, you know that,' he says. 'Besides I think he was already dead by the time I got there. His body was lifeless when I lifted him. There was no breathing.'

'What I know and what you know does not appear to matter to my daughter. "Why did he bother to save me?" She asks me the same question every morning when she wakes. "And leave me like this? Why did he not just leave me there to die with Angelo?" That's what she says, Paul. "Then I would've thanked him from the grave."'

They are back at the villa. She has slipped into a bikini and bathrobe and he is doing more preliminary sketches of her as she relaxes on the sunlounge, a glass of red wine in her hand.

'I was never really very brave,' he says

'If that is so, what made you act as you did? I mean you hardly knew my daughter.'

'True.' He ponders holding his pencil still. 'I acted rashly but my action was perhaps more for you. At least that is what I thought at the time. That I was helping you by saving your daughter.'

'You did not even know me.'

'Maybe it was my way of trying to get to know you. Of gaining an entry as it were.'

'Ha, as it were.' She places the wine on the small glass table and lifts her bikini top. You like my breasts?'

Paul stalls. 'They... have perfect symmetry.'

'Ha-ha. Perfect symmetry.'

'They are beautiful in fact.'

'Bashful old man, you are blushing. You think they are real?'

'I don't know, are they?'

She smiles. 'Does it matter once they achieve the desired effect? Think of the senses.'

'Am I not already obsessed by one of those? Weighed down by it? Seeing comes before words. As a child I saw and recognised my mother in her robing and disrobing before I could speak.'

'And what effect did that have on you?'

'I don't know, maybe something subliminal.'

'So you can fashion her in your mind now to your heart's content with your pencils and brushes.'

'My earliest doodlings were of curves. Mountains and rivers,'

'And women.'

'Yes, eventually.'

'Eventually, ha. You're still getting around to women, aren't you?'

He examines his dripping brush as if for an answer. 'Perhaps I am. It's all a mystery, isn't it, these atavistic impulses? There are parts of our makeup I suppose which we will never know.'

'Lighten up señor,' she says reaching for her vape. 'Who wants to know everything and, besides, there are other senses apart from seeing. Like touch.'

'Yes.'

'Touch me here,' she says offering her left breast.

She sees him hesitating.

'Go on.'

He touches her breast with a cautious index figure.

She laughs. 'My dear Pablo, don't you know how to hold a woman's breast? You have to cup it in your hand. Oh, I should not be laughing with the state of my daughter. Perhaps you think I should be in sackcloth, that we should not be doing this sort of thing, but you do make me laugh.'

'Humour was also one of the suppressed joys.'

'Where? Oh yes, you mean in your institution. Pablo, you are such an innocent.' She watches him as he feels the soft pulp inside his palm. 'Well, what is your artistic appraisal?'

'Have I said that before?'

'What?'

'About fruit?'

'It's a cliché. Why are we women like fruit?'

'Because of your fecundity I suppose.'

'Ha. Fecundity. The words you come up with.'

'Soft,' he says growing bolder as he allows his hand to linger, 'like the mellifluence of your voice, although at other times that voice of yours can be — '

'Harsh, I know.'

'Like when you are talking to the maid.'

'That is just me, the many parts of me.'

'That time,' he says, 'you called my name in the sea breeze.'

'That was teasing.'

'Yes maybe that's all it was but soft nonetheless.'

'Imagine Pablo, what a woman can do for a man.'

'Please enlighten me.'

'Tomorrow I will show you one of my films so you will pick up a few tips.'

'Tips?'

'It's just a manner of speaking. They were all film noir you know, my films, well mostly. Funny that they rarely saw me in a romantic role. Sexy and sultry yes, but not romantic. Dangerous was a word someone used about me. That I projected danger.'

You are dangerous, he thinks but he changes the subject. 'Your daughter,' he says, 'you treat her as if she is an encumbrance, an unwanted appendage.'

'We can only talk for ourselves, each one of us. Daughter or mother, what difference does it make, we are all just individual atoms floating about, aren't we? It takes all one's time just to look after oneself. Isn't that the way to be, the only way to be for the short span it lasts for a woman.'

'And what about an ageing man? Me, for instance?'

'You can still satisfy your desire, Pablo. What I mean is, until a woman's looks are gone to excite the man, she must use whatever attributes she has to get what she wants.'

'And what do you want, Viviana?'

'We are in this world for a purpose, Paul. You are an artist and I am an actress. It is our destiny. They don't understand.'

'Who are they?'

'Javier and village illiterates, and even my late father. They don't understand what acting is. It is a way of freeing oneself from the prison inside ourselves. By becoming someone else, someone beautiful and admired, oh yes, but most of all free. Being an actress means one has to draw nourishment from the varieties of life.'

'You mean by not being monogamous, like playing around, is that what they call it?'

She laughs. 'Playing around, what an innocent phrase. The Americans make it all sound so innocent, don't they? But it's loaded, isn't it?'

'Yes it is loaded.'

'Wherever there is nourishment Pablo, one must draw from it. Nothing must stand in the way of our destiny.'

'So you believe in destiny.'

'Oh yes. But the reality right at this moment is I am an obscure actress being kept in the dark by a restrictive force, and you Paul are unknown as yet. So both of us need to emerge from the darkness, and we can help one another to do that. I become famous. Your painting of me becomes famous. We both win.'

'And how exactly do you propose we go about that?' he says.

She does not speak but takes from her beach bag which was lying on the tiles the pearled revolver.

He rises, puts away his pencils. 'I better go.'

'Are you frightened, Pablo?'

He does not answer, pretending not to hear her shouting after him: 'Great hero and warrior,' as he exits.

***

The following morning he returns rather peevishly but drawn nonetheless. He had spent a sleepless night trying to overcome his reservations and fears concerning this lady, but determined to see his project through, accepting whatever delays or circuitous routes it may take. Leaving his easel and paints and brushes down as instructed, he sits beside her on the sofa in her large, white-tiled sitting room. The curtains are pulled across and he feels as if he is about to be given a lesson in some nefarious action on how to murder. She huddles close beside him, her long tanned legs protruding from a midnight blue robe. He senses a stirring in himself sitting so close to her, and she, noticing with a downward glance towards the protuberance in his crotch, knows she has a power over him. The film noir *Last Breath* in its dark setting more black than white is showing as a DVD on a large TV screen.

'Maribel,' she whispers, 'is sleeping now after another restless night.'

'Good,' he says not knowing what much else to add.

The setting is in a casino. Viviana in tight black skirt is rolling the roulette wheel. There are several men in tuxedos and bow ties standing around the table She has a cigarette elongated in a slender bakelite holder in the corner of her mouth with smoke snaking out of it. A tall man with greasy back-combed hair is winning every time at the wheel. He does not look at her, but one senses a frisson between them as he gathers the chips, his winnings, and gives them to her, a great mountain of chips which she fills into a sack closed with a diamond-topped cord.

The film moves to a different scene. A hotel bedroom. Viviana is at her vanity mirror combing her straight black fringed hair with an ivory comb. The same man, now bare-chested showing a Brillo pad of hair, is reclining on a bed propped up by a couple of pillows. The camera focuses on his beady eyes taking her in. He beckons with his hand for her to come to him. His lips move but he says nothing.

'There is no sound,' Paul says.

'Of course not,' Viviana says. 'I have turned the volume down.'

'But why?'

'Pablo,' she says caressing his thigh, is it not the role of the artist to imagine?'

She fast-forwards, her long red nailed fingers pressing the remote control, pointing it like a weapon towards the screen.

The movie continues with a shot of the garish lights of Las Vegas (or what purports to be Las Vegas) caught through the window of the hotel bedroom. She is still wearing that tight black skirt with high heels. She looks so slim, so one dimensional as she sits on the side of a kingsize bed and opens a white leather handbag. She takes out a small pistol. It is similar to the pearl-handled weapon she had shown him. She checks the barrel for the bullet. And quickly looks up as if startled towards the door. She has just time enough to return the pistol to the hand bag when the door opens. A man enters, the same man who had won all the money at the casino. He looks angry judging by his lips; it appears he is shouting at Viviana. He approaches her with clenched fists. Viviana cowers down before him muttering something. His height is imposing now, doubled by the vanity mirror. He strikes her a mighty blow, sending her reeling across the floor, the handbag caught in her arm landing beside her. He comes towards her again. She reaches for the handbag and, as his large bulk is about to come down on her, she takes out the pistol and shoots him straight in the face.

'Very violent,' Paul says

'Does it shock you?'

'It would if it were real. I would've liked to have heard you speaking.'

'The pistol spoke. Was that not enough? I was a gang's moll. I could be shared and dispensed with, you understand. But I wasn't really a moll at all, that's the thing. These producers think they own you and can do anything they like with you. They think you are the same sultry actress on the screen as off the screen. But I was clever, *entiendes*? Their heist, the money they stole from the casino, from the roulette wheel was rigged by me.'

'I figured that,' he says.

'And I was the mole meant to remove the money, but they forgot one thing, didn't they? They presumed I was going to give it back to them.'

He isn't sure if Viviana is acting out her role or extemporising.

'A B movie star, I hear one of them say. That is all I was yes, all B movies, how a lot of actresses started but never got to A. That's where my husband entered the scene. He prevented me from going from B to A. Don't you understand, Paul, he was that villain.'

Paul wonders and, not for the first time, if Viviana is unhinged. When she pauses the film to go to the bathroom, he seizes the controls and raises the volume. The actors are speaking in Spanish.

Watching a blue moth fluttering like a speck of paper in a breeze landing on a geranium but fickle and transient, flitting away to some new delight, the beauty of it. They are outside again by the heart-shaped pool. She is sitting on her sunbed facing him, holding her pashmina around her shoulders now as there is a breeze as he sketches: another attempt at her eyebrows.

'How long will it live,' he says, 'the moth?'

'Oh Pablo,' she says noticing his diverted gaze, 'don't waste your time with such trifling. Tell me what was it like in that reformatory of yours?'

'Of mine? Hardly mine. And it wasn't a reformatory, it was a seminary.'

'Whatever,' she says. 'Did you eat well? It's so important to eat well.'

And he thinks of her recent indifference to whether her daughter ate or not.

'There were gardens which we tended and which provided fresh vegetables, and there were hens running about, the only free agents in that cloistered world.'

'Free range eggs. That was good, surely. Free-thinking hens,' she scoffs.

'A boiled egg every morning in a metal eggcup.'

'Did you say mental eggcup?'

'No, a metal eggcup served by a harassed looking local woman who came and went like some shadowy creature. I never got to know her. She disappeared soon after I arrived and the room, the refectory as it was called, took on an even gloomier appearance like chrome and polished shoes and...'

'What are you doing?' he asks, for he feels uncomfortable as her stare pierces him.

'I'm practising my Giaconda gaze. *Le regard.* It is my turn. I am the starer. I am the one now who ogles. Let's turn it on its head, this male gaze thing. You are just a voyeur, Pablo.'

'A voyeur? Really? But is that not the way of it? Girls wear short skirts and high heels when sometimes they do not even feel comfortable in such dress. So why do they do it? Hardly for the female gaze, hardly for themselves. They want to attract the male, like the female moth shedding its scent.'

'You think you have the answers, ha.'

'That's the way of it in my estimation at least,' he says no longer caring if she is mocking him or not, 'the biological propensity that can't be cauterised by misandrist rhetoric.'

'Whoa. Slow down old man, that's a mouthful.'

'You know what I believe about those misandrists? I believe they are frustrated sexually.'

'Perhaps like you, Pablo. Are you frustrated sexually?'

'I suppose I am.'

'The world has fucked both of us up in our different ways, hasn't it, Paul?'

'In different ways,' he repeats, as if he is tasting the words.

'Totally,' she says, 'and look at you, old man.'

'Old man.'

'Young in vigour'. She draws breath making her breasts rise. 'I really like you, you know, and I don't find you old at all. It's just a phrase Pablo, a manner of speaking.'

9

The following morning, while entering through the French doors, he finds Viviana by the pool talking with her back to him on her mobile phone. 'Bene.' He overhears the Italian word quietly spoken He is about to consider leaving and coming in again, when she turns.

Paul, head down, busies himself preparing his palette, pretending not to have heard anything.

'You enter like a mouse,' she says.

'Sorry,' he says, 'I didn't realise—'

'He wants her back in Madrid.'

'Who?'

'Who do you think was on the phone, *el señor ministro*.'

Once more he is puzzled by her lie. Javier would not be speaking to his wife in Italian and also it is unlikely she would be speaking so softly to someone she professes to despise.

'He says the doctors will be better able to look after her there. You know these *madrileños*, they think they are the bees knees. There is talk of an operation. If she is to get it, it would be better in Madrid, he says. And of course she wants to go herself, to be with her papá,' she adds sourly, 'but I don't know if it is for the best.'

Glad to be rid of her, he feels like saying, for that he presumes is Viviana's estimation of her daughter, enfeebled or not. Instead he says 'There would be better facilities in Madrid surely to look after her, I mean.'

'Oh let them be at whatever they want to be at,' she snaps, 'I'm going for a shower.'

He is drawing a mouth, curved, top lip darker, corners tucked in softer and cooler. Pouting lips, dark and pale pink twisted slantways ever so slightly below the bridge of her nose and the spheres of her eyes gazing from their sockets.

'A mocking mouth,' she says leaning over him. She is holding a towel around her after her shower and the tips of her wet tussled hair brush sensuously against the back of his neck.

'Me?'

'Of course.'

'I like it,' she says, 'I like the mocking tone.'

'Four years it took da Vinci to manufacture that gaze.'

'He was vain. He just wanted us to look at his own face.'

'Do I highlight the sexuality, your sexuality I mean or merely your geometric dimensions? Is that part of my problem in following Da Vinci?'

'Your adverb, Pablo, has answered your question. You want all of me, don't you, not an anatomical part. I must admit though I like the mocking mouth. I want to be viewed as one who mocks the world's absurdities.'

'But that will not necessarily be my desire.'

She sighs. 'Oh Pablo. You are becoming tiresome. Can we not develop, negotiate, something in-between?'

'Compromise dilutes passion.' And he can't believe he is saying these things, talking like this from some occluded cavern inside himself.

'Not a compromise then, a sort of mutual desire. I have a suggestion on how to start.'

'You do?'

She takes a phial from her handbag which is resting by her sunbed. 'Drink it,' she says.

'What is it?'

'Something to make you a stranger to yourself.'

And he thinks maybe it is something her doctor prescribes or some drug unknown to him.

'Oh Pablo, my artist,' she says laughing. 'Take your clothes off for gods sake. How can you paint another's body when you cannot feel your own?'

Removing her towel she mounts the sunbed positioning her derrière knowingly, having slanted protuberantly in the primordial way. She turns her head, smiling and watches, the effrontery of the gaze giving her authority over him.

The phone rings vibrating on the glass table.

'Aren't you going to answer it?'

'Leave it,' she says.

'Don't you think it may be important, about Maribel perhaps?'

'I know who it is. Ignore it. Take the phial.'

The phone rings out and she watches him swallow the phial with the dark chestnut of her smiling come-hither eye drawing him on. The zip of his chinos he opens, pulling down and the boxers he stalls on—perhaps he could work in those but her pouting says, *Adelante* and he peels off to reveal the bobbing instrument encased in a mound of grey hair. He instructs himself to no longer feel embarrassed or ashamed but emboldened, and to feel the curtailment of all the years encapsulated in this, his member, released now throbbing under her gaze.

'You know when I attended art classes we women were not allowed to view the male models in *deshabille*.'

'I never—'

'So you see in portraying the nude body, it is not equal pegging.'

'Perhaps I should—'

'Don't you know Pablo, the world consists of those who look and those who look away. Let me watch you *hacerte una paja*.'

'Sorry?'

'Spank the monkey.'

After he makes a gestured effort on the flaccid member she says, 'You are not able to do it?'

'Too much conditioning I suppose, like it should be a secretive act or something intrinsically wrong.'

'Bishops do it.'

'How do you know?'

'How do I know anything? Where is your dog collar?'

'You know I no longer have such a thing.'

'But you carry the residue, right? All that constraining stuff that you talk of. You are free now, Pablo, free with me.'

He turns his gaze away from her feeling a blush coming on.

'Pablo.'

'I feel I am regressing to adolescence.'

'You are an adolescent in that area. Do you want me to help?' She arches her body catlike.

'I used to cross my hands.'

'What?'

'When we were in the dormitories.'

'When you were growing excited?'

'Over my heart when I went to bed, entangled in the chains of my rosary beads.'

'Interesting you should equate chains and beads.'

'To ward off evil.'

'Evil?'

'Despite...'

'Yes...?

'The sounds from the neighbouring beds.'

'What sounds, Paul?'

'You called me Paul? Like I am two persons.'

'Was he not a sinner before he was a saint? The opposite to you, Pablo. Look at it,' she says with mocking eyes, 'you think you are great, what you hold in your hand, you think it is the universe and it makes you great. You are pathetic,' she says and reaches for her towel.

'I never wept over things that life brought,' he says feeling the moisture in his eyes now like a small boy being caught out for doing something naughty.

'You are quite overcome now, aren't you, Paul?'

'Sorry.' He sniffles.

'There is no need to apologise.'

'You must excuse me,' he says.

'What are a few tears, Pablo, in the great pool of life? Do you think,' she says looking down at him, 'your little drops will be noticed? How helpless desire is in you males. How feeble you are.'

She stares at him in ridicule. Nevertheless, even despite realising this, the power she exerts over him, prevents him from walking away. This slow build-up of control which she was able to mould through the sex of her gender ever since they first met, has trapped him. And the way she regards him now so fearlessly. He feels embarrassed without any cover of darkness to conceal the state he is in, exposed in his nakedness. Never before had he stood in such a manner in front of another human in full light. She turns knowing the way it arouses him with the mid-day sun reflecting off the glass of the French door dazzling him. And she, the beholder of him, a woman of such astounding beauty. Would he ever have dreamed of such a thing? And did it happen, this seeping? He gropes for his shirt, any garment will do, and looks to her under his eyes, having to ask, like that small boy in him again grovelling, if he can use the shower.

And afterwards, 'You celibate,' she says and laughs, 'what a joke. It is this desire that seems to posses you, Paul. It is woman's power. And you are right, those misandrists who scare you, fail to realise their power lies not in academic tract or shrill denouncements but in sex and allure, the giving and the withholding, to make the man dependent. Is that not power? The man like a dog or a slave salivating, bowing down in adoration. That is where the female power lies over the male.'

And, as she continues laughing, he feels duped. He has been duped by trusting in her, by revealing his vulnerability to her, for it is only now he realises that it is that vulnerability which is providing her with the pleasure. That hidden secret thing that was never meant to happen, not with all those upstanding saintly personages failing, giving in to the so-called baser instincts— the subject of endless salacious confessions.

'Don't you know,' she is saying when you strip away all those things that are bothering one, when one is raw— '

'Raw?'

'Yes, when we are like that, we are impelled to behave in a certain way, and that's the truth of ourselves.'

'You know about truth?'

'I know about raw. All the other ways are just constructs, so if I want to, let us say, kill a man...'

'Kill?'

'Yes. That is being raw, that is being true to one's raw self. And what happened between us just now was a mere precursor to what we can really do, you and I Paul, together.'

He does not feel good. He feels humiliated, used, abused. Why did she want him to do that? While she looked on. Is it some kind of voyeurism that is in her, or is it control and power she is after? But despite those (conditioned?) feelings of shame, there is a peculiar compulsion, a magnetic attraction to her words of command and, in succumbing to her will, the whiff of a delicious outrage.

PART II

10

Released the Spring day of his emancipation (the dog collar surrendered) from the order holding the small cardboard suitcase in one hand and the incongruity of a potted plant in his other. There it was glistening before him: the world of nature, the sweet smell of the buddleia overhanging the cloistered wall drawing him, impregnating his nostrils with delightful scent, banishing all those musty book smells of the past. He visited his mother's grave before he departed for Spain on the little hillside graveyard in West Cork where she came from and where people used to joke almost in cliché form about the great view the corpses would have of the mountains, and he fondled the soft crumbly soil of the resurrected earth wafting with the new scent of lavender. And in the evening when he alighted from the plane and approached the *piso*, the scent of orange late blossoming and growing wild and free in an open space was beguiling and intoxicating him and filled him with such overflowing pleasure that he thought his heart was going to burst. It was like it was saying, You silly boy, look what you've missed, all those years, all those sterile years, and Brother Marías, an almost pathologically shy and sensitive man who gave you the potted plant. His voice could be heard from his room talking sweetly to his plants, all of whose names he knew and addressed in Latin and that he nurtured as if they were his loving offspring. And the potted plant of which he was most proud a *Robinia Frisia pseudocacia inermis*— without thorns, without the thorns of Christ, he entrusted to Paul, something to carry through the universe to show that something could exist pure, unpierced, unarmed without pain or predation, grown from seed, cultivated with loving words, that was something to show for all the years of barrenness. Sow the seeds of love, he would say. Plant them in the spring. Keep that in memory of me, Pablo, he said and maybe the white flowers will bloom in it, the white flower that refused to bloom in this country because it needs more sun. And

Paul thought it was like a parody of the Christ speaking at the Last Supper, Do this in memory of me.

Paul had opted for Spain because Brother Marías, whose people had come from the old Moorish village of A—, in his lucid moments had taught him his first words of Spanish. It was a natural follow-up to the indoctrinated Latin, and he spoke of Spain frequently and he said in your reading of its history to ignore the inquisition and Franco and their exaggerated festive pageants, and if you can do that, the land will liberate you and give you new life because it is the land of Helios.

Paul had hoped that the Cuban landlady, Señora Mendoza, who resides on the ground floor, would not object to the presence of his plant, for it is something to inspire him and remind him of his old friend whose life was not in vain as long as he beheld the plant. That landlady now he thinks, she could teach him about women in a mature way perhaps without the inherent danger presented by Viviana. She had left a welcoming yellow rose for him on his kitchen table in a glass vase suggesting what? Preferential treatment or a kindness at least, for she seemed to have taken to him in a matronly way. She was twenty three years now living in Spain but still with a house back in Havana rented by her cousin. She didn't like students. She told him she had many students staying in the summer months bedding some three in a room. 'Fornicating. Oh yes. Those American college students 'doing' Europe on the cheap are the worst offenders. You can hear their sexual groans and grunts throughout the night, but you señor, you are an *estimado* señor, and I have a quiet room for you, for your reflective self. You don't mind my saying that señor, for you remind me, forgive me, but you remind me of a padre in the quiet civil way you have about you. But there are alas so few men like that now, men of the cloth prepared to sacrifice their life for a supreme goal, not like these young fornicators that think of nothing else other than satisfying their fleshly desires. But they will pass, señor. I have been here many years since the Cuban revolution. I have seen them come and go like perennial flowers señor, coming and going with their different hairstyles and fashions and their cutaway jeans, but deep down they're are all the same, thinking they are discovering the world for the first time, thinking they are unique. But they are not unique. In fact they are tiresome, showing off, quoting philosophers and writers. Who is in and who is out. They think they are of the moment. True originators, they have just arrived and the world is new to them. How utterly trivial they are. It is all passing señor, but they don't know that. But they pay me. I take their money. I have to survive, don't I? I can tell you about poverty, señor. Don't get me started.'

The señora had no objection to the plant; in fact she admired it, and Paul thought sadly of his friend whom he never addressed by his first name without the chained prefix; such familiarity was frowned upon in the Congregation: the only one you can be familiar with is god.

It is late evening and he has invited Viviana to dine with him in *La Cuchara*. He wanted to get her away from the villa or more particularly to get himself away too (all buildings are incarcerations in their own right) for a while at least after the previous day's trauma. He is still not quite sure how to fathom what happened or didn't happen, to make sense of his 'freezing' at that moment. All those musings about conditioning and freedom and how he thought he had his life figured out rationally and then, when it came to the crunch as it were, everything crumbled under her gaze. Or could it have been the damn prostate interfering into the scheme of thing? But how bold she was, how utterly daring for a woman to do what she did, to make fun of him like he was a mere marionette to her, whose strings she could pull at will. It is as if—and a shudder seizes him—instead of being free he is being conditioned in a new way, as if he is being moulded for a purpose. But what purpose? Still, it is comforting, he thinks looking around, to be out and about among people who are eating and drinking and getting on with their lives. It gives one at least a temporary reprieve, to escape intensity and recuperate as it were.

The daytime eatery is now transformed into a candlelit restaurant with starched laundered tablecloths and serviettes replacing the utilitarian paper ones used for lunches. Viviana had made it clear to him that some nights were not free and she had limited time to dedicate to this famous painting as she called it but she could 'fit him in' this Thursday evening. The waiter on duty is a different fellow from the daytime one, more polished with slick hair. He greets them or rather her like royalty, holding the chair for her, smiling ingratiatingly. 'It is indeed an honour señora,' and Paul feels self-conscious for here he is in the presence of a celebrated actress as if he is part of a movie set, and he notices in Viviana a delight in this reverence, this adulation being showered on her in one of her public appearances. But that is only the perception she wants to create, for she has appeared so many times out and about, and the waiter is just being polite. And she shows it in the flaunting of her sheer body-hugging black dress, her head held high, telling the world she is somebody, an entitled one, a goddess who would never have to lower herself into the drab little world of mortals.

'Maribel has gone,' she says in a deadpan voice when the waiter withdraws. Her smile also withdraws and he realises it is a show, a flash like the camera lights on the sets. 'Yes, that is why I am free tonight. Her father has taken her back to Madrid. It appears she is to attend some eminent eye surgeon.'

'Perhaps it is for the best.'

'At least it will give us some time to sort out things.'

'What things?'

'Oh Paul, be patient. Besides, who knows? Maybe with time away from us she may come around to think on you differently.'

'That is to be hoped for.'

'But not of me,' she quickly adds, 'she will never change her opinion of me. Anyway for now,' she says adjusting her serviette on her lap, 'let us leave unpleasant matters.'

He looks at her as she breaks bread and, with its rough edges, dips it into the olive oil on her salad plate.

'I like the Spanish way,' he says.

'The Spanish way?'

'It should always be the breaking of the bread. It is more Biblical. Christ broke the bread which is a hint of real lives, of a pre-institutionalised church rather than the geometrically accurate knife slicing of a regimental upbringing.'

There is such a drawn seriousness in her face 'We are broken, Pablo. All of us are broken.'

'What do you mean?'

'I mean life breaks us into crumbs. That's all we are, crumbs I could've been—'

'I know,' he says touching her hand, sensing her emotion, that momentary faltering in the voice, something he had not noticed before.

She releases her hand and takes a tablet from her handbag as a darkness descends on her. And he notices, as she swallows with a glass of water, her eyes losing their texture, the left one differing from the other: one dark cruel eye harsh staring, the other, the softer chocolaty melting eye that had bewitched him the first time he beheld her.

'The loaves and the fishes ha,' she says when the waiter comes with the fried cod.

'I don't mind,' he says, 'your ridiculing of religion. It doesn't matter to me anymore, but the point is still there.'

'What point?'

'That there is not enough.'

'And some have too much like me, isn't that what you're implying?'

'Perhaps.'

'It's the system Pablo, the capitalist system you're talking about.'

He sighs. 'I mean the historical Christ wanted to break down that system to show a different way.'

'I thought you were finished with religion.'

'Maybe I am, but not the system.'

'Ha.'

After the meal he reaches for the bill

She pushes his hand away.

'We don't pay, Paul. Javier pays.'

11

It is early morning. He is carrying his easel and cotton bag as they walk towards the beach. No prying eyes, the way she likes it. He would have preferred some dunes to protect them from the easterly wind but there are no dunes on this coast. 'You have to go to Portugal for the dunes,' she says. 'We will make the best of it.' He wants to catch the early light, to portray her with the first of the sunshine to illumine her face, to concentrate on capturing her eyes under that blue oil colour that becomes a sky before cloud encroachment which had the habit of happening in the afternoon during the last few days. Oh, and also to avoid the hordes of sunseekers who would be appearing later, commandeering sunbeds and space.

'The Giaconda's eyes did not match, did you know that, Pablo?'

They have stopped at a spot remote from road and people. Nobody's eyes match. And he thinks about her eyes not matching and wonders about his own. He had never examined them close up in a mirror. If there was a difference, it would be minimal.

She removes her white sandals as they leave the path, holding onto him for support to balance, the action filling him with pleasure.

'This repayment business,' she says, holding her sandals now in one hand by their straps, 'is going on quite a bit.'

'You agreed.'

'I know that, but we must make progress.'

'How can you put a time limit on art?'

'That sounds pompous.'

'It's developing.'

'Like our relationship.'

'You could say.'

She squeezes his arm. 'Did all artists forge intimacies with their models?'

'Some did.'

'The lechers.'

'Consensual lechery.'

She laughs. 'Oh Pablo, you have well and truly buried your collar now.'

'It is black comedy you are playing at,' he says as she settles on her Helios towel, 'using me as a kind of pawn in some plan you have. It is a plan, isn't it?'

She places a finger on his parted lips. And then as if to change the subject says, 'All the sketches and paintings you do, without touching.'

'Without touching?'

Has she forgotten how she had previously asked him to touch her breasts? It's like each day is a new beginning for her, starting with a new slate wiped clean.

'You just touch the canvas. Is that enough for you, Paul? How do you get that texture of me? Don't you want to touch me, the mortal one?'

Perhaps he understands her now, that this is the moment, she is telling him with that glint in her eye. She is about to fulfil his desire not merely visually but offering more, by telling him to leave the brush down to come to her as she reclines O'Murphy style on her towel. He obeys, wipes away a smudge of paint from his fingers with a cloth, and approaches hesitantly but with rising excitement. Never before had he behaved in such a manner in an open, public space. Is this real? Is this happening? This beautiful woman enticing, inviting a man nearly double her age to enjoy her. Is it some sort of fantasy long delayed surfacing from the deep recesses of his subconscious? An erotic dream, a wish fulfilment. He fumbles with the belt of his pants.

'I am waiting, Pablo. You are too slow old man.'

'Sorry I...'

She turns and reaches for her robe. 'How will I ever teach you? You are just too slow.'

What was it, he wondered afterwards, the cause of his dilatoriness? The fear of someone passing by, the sound of guilt on the roar of the waves. Her forwardness, her brazenness, a brazen hussy, he had heard the word on men's lips in Dublin pubs. And his mother had used the phrase once about some forward girl in the community. Where was Eros or the demureness he loved in women spawning a mystery? And he concluded: mystery is an essential ingredient of desire. Not mystery about her past but about her makeup. The ideal was broken. Viviana is just ordinary. Vulgar in fact, that is the word.

***

Recovered from the slight, he is engrossed now in the painting. He has removed his shirt and moved from the eyebrows and is trying to capture her nose, not sharp and pointed like the aquiline noses of the classical period, and which he had never liked in so many books of religious art, but soft and smooth pastels he uses and pale colours and more individual than the patrician ladies of ancient Rome who all seemed to have had the same nose. But this individual nose now is not too small or bulbous, but petite with the hint of pertness in its slight upturnedness. It is coming along fine, well at least more to his satisfaction than his efforts heretofore. He is forgetting the time as the sun rises and that little breeze of early morning has abated, and Viviana it seems is quite happy to indulge in the pleasant heat, her sallow skin already tanned.

'It is near midday Pablo, time for lunch.'

'Yes, yes,' he says excitedly. He can feel the heat burning down on him, but he can't stop now. He has mastered what he wants to portray. He must finish the nose after its long development from pencil to chalk and the most delicate of brush strokes.

It is only when he has returned to her villa and showered that he sees himself in the long wall mirror and realises his chest and shoulders are as red as beetroot.

She berates him for his folly. 'Don't you know the sun like the sea like fire, you as an artist should know the elements.'

The elements yes, he thought he knew those and Helios in particular whom upto this at least he felt he was befriending. And then he goes and mistreats him like that with a burning, a searing, that was not the act of a friend. Perhaps he was trying to tell Paul something, that he was embarking on the wrong course, that he needs to take stock. Just a little bolt of disapproval, that's all the sunburn was.

She insists on tending to his burns and surprisingly shows great solicitude towards him (in contrast to what she shows towards her daughter or maid) which makes him think that maybe it was worth getting the burn to enjoy the after-effects of her gentle caresses as she administers the aloe vera.

'You pale Celtic creatures,' she says, 'need to be careful in the sun.'

He is lying on the double bed (the matrimonial bed?) in fawn cotton shorts, the fading light shimmering through the gossamer curtains. The aloe vera is soothing, her hand gliding softly over his chest. To lie, he thinks, somewhat uncomfortably, in the hollow where someone else had lain. Who was his predecessor other than her husband? That is if he did share it, perhaps he was banished, her odium so strong. But what about other lovers referred to by Maribel? Is their lust still contaminating the sheets? Did they really exist? This mysterious Benito, was he here? He feels the satin sheet under him as if it is defiled?

'And another thing,' she says, 'you should get a van Gogh hat. He was not as mad as you when it came to the sun.'

***

What does it contain? Viviana comes to view it, the work in progress, propped on its easel by the pool.

'I am not in it,' she exclaims, 'I am not there at all.'

'Not yet.'

'Just bits of me.'

Using fingers as a smudge tool. Subtracting colour, keeping the nose, deleting the contentious eyebrow, pulling light back, reclaiming it. The shape of a shadow.

'How I hate Caravaggio,' he says.

And he thinks of his early cloistered drawings of dark corridors and dormitories with steel bedposts. Steel. Unbreakable. How many were broken in those beds?

'I wrote an essay on him,' she says.

'What, on Caravaggio? In Italy I presume.'

'Yes. A colour also has a shape, remember. The shape of colour.'

'The painting has to be the image of what was,' he says, 'the ideal, the perfect form before the desired bits start to quiver a little more than normal.'

'My bits?'

'Anybody's bits.'

'And what is normal? You think I'm normal?'

'I don't know. Are you?'

'Some people think I'm not.'

'Like who?'

'The gadfly, the daughter. They think...'

'What?'

'Never mind.' She shrugs. 'So,' she says reaching for her ecig, 'you're not after me at all but rather the ideal, what never really is.'

'You are deconstructing the myth.'

'Ah, you admit it is all a myth then, this searching for perfect form.'

'Not really. For its worth, for what I can make of it in my limited experience that is. Maybe it is not a myth, but something indefinable.'

'Ha, the bearded woman in the circus, is she indefinable or desirable? Or the former beauty now with her rounded belly and varicose veins?'

He turns from her. 'Please don't tell me such things.'

'Why? Do they spoil your illusion? Menstruations perhaps.'

'Please.'

'A turnoff. Why don't you say it? You don't know anything about women do you, Paul?'

'No,' he says and he is suddenly conscious of his own discomfort with the prostate which has surfaced suddenly.

'Like all men you haven't a clue, deep down.'

She stares at him as if she is undressing him, penetrating to his very bones. 'I know what you want, Paul. What you want is is the equivalent of a Constable landscape without the cow dung. You are limited Pablo, you will never capture a complete woman.'

'That is the point,' he says, resting his brush. 'Perhaps the painting is not meant to be finished.'

'How can you say such a thing? You think I can loiter around here all my life at your beck and call for something that will never end.'

'Perhaps it must be perpetually evolving like homo sapiens, because...'

'Because what?'

'Because when the painting is finished, I fear our relationship may also end with it.'

'Just get on with it, will you for god sake.'

'I mean as long as things keep happening.'

'Things?'

'Our mutual desires.'

'You think I desire you. You flatter yourself.'

'I mean desires not necessarily for me.'

'All right then,' she says reaching for her vape. 'What you want are colours: mellow anode glowing like droplets of gold and brushwork, loose a la Titian.'

'Titian?'

'He is the Helios you seek, Paul.'

'Perhaps, but as long as I keep adding new brushstrokes...'

'That is only a hope, an *anhelo*.'

'I am trying to inject a meaning into all these squares and rectangles.'

'What about the circles?'

'Yes of course, you would say that, wouldn't you.'

'But that is what we are doing you and I, isn't it, going around in circles?'

'Plotinus says the soul adores the circle.'

'There you go with that soul again.'

'Like the world.'

'Ha, the world,' she says. 'Let me ask you is the perceptual expression also a spiritual one for you, Pablo, after all, considering your background?'

'Well of course, if you are perceiving a religious painting.'

'But not just religious surely.'

'The woman creating a—'

'What about the woman?' she says sharply interrupting him, 'this imagined creature of yours from the incarceration of the cloister creating a fantasy in your mind.'

'It is not just the erotic or the material or the worldly for that matter which one's mind, in contrast to one's body, seems to inhabit. No, it is not that but the canvas on which I will paint you. You will be worshipped not as a cold human who cares not for her daughter, but as a goddess. Isn't that what you aspire to be?'

'Surely that is dishonest, Paul. How can I be a cold human or a goddess? You can't have both. Make up your mind. Which way do you want me? You really believe I am a cold human. We are all capable of coldness.'

'I accept that. But the other side, the goddess in you, that is what I am trying to capture.'

'Your ideal of woman, your ideal of god. What's the difference? *Mulier est templum oedificatur super cloacam* was a phrase of my father's borrowed from Tertulian.'

'I have not heard of it.'

'Woman is a temple built over a sewer.'

'What a statement.'

'Yes, I must say it didn't do my self-esteem any good on hearing that. Left me wondering what my father really thought of me, and when I asked him to explain he just said, Look it up, educate yourself.'

She turns to him with pleading in her eyes for the first time. 'Oh Pablo, don't you know all ideals come tumbling down eventually. Don't, Pablo. Don't mount such a high horse. You are just a designer.'

'That is the supreme insult.'

'No Pablo. I don't mean to insult you.'

'Not only to me but to what went before us, the tradition: Michelangelo, da Vinci, were they merely great designers?'

'It's all a sham,' she says. 'Who is the best trickster, the most convincing? The one who commands the biggest payroll.'

12

He strips naked before the long mirror. He lifts away all that apparel, all those hefts and collars that had weighed him down and the suffocating mask, he breathes deeply the sweet warm air wafting in from the balcony with the saline smell from the sea hearing the companionable roar of the waves. You are just flesh and bone, Saint Jerome without the saint prefix or the brandished cross, bones withering, flesh and cerebrum unfettered, unhampered, and the prostate lurking behind the dangling bit, the source of it all. Stand there now and behold the transformation, the falling away of leaves that gathered blocking the shores. Step out from yourself like a snake sloughing off its skin. Leave the old, wrinkled skin behind and come to the desired one and be free.

'You are holding me too tightly.'

'Sorry,' he says releasing his grip from her shoulder.

In the cool evening they are reclining under a duvet on the summer marriage bed. She so confidently with so much sangfroid of bodily proximity and he lying wondering, fidgeting, what is he supposed to do, what does she expect him to do, this lady beside him now, beautiful in all aspects, the apotheosis of woman and he blessed anointed, so fortunate to be lying down here beside her. And she *is* interested in him, a white-haired ageing man. And when he enquires of Javier, she says, 'Off somewhere, pretending to be doing business for the government but more likely visiting his decrepit father in Tarragona.'

She touches his shoulder. 'You have very strong hands, you realise that?'

'I forget that sometimes.'

'Never mind. They may become useful.'

'Useful?'

'You never committed, did you Paul, holy man?'

'You are mocking me.'

'It will be all the sweeter. The holy man doing the deed.'

'What deed?'

'Hear me out. And you will have me then, the source of your desire. It's what you want, isn't it, Paul? All your life has been building up to this moment without your even knowing it. Our coming together, it's destiny.'

She proffers the gun from under the duvet. 'Take it, Paul. Play with it. Familiarise yourself with it. It is the dessert.'

She throws off the duvet revealing her naked breasts and black laced panties. 'What can you not let go of? What hurts you the most?'

What hurts him the most? What can he say, caressing a revolver and averting his eyes but only slightly, more bold now is he becoming in the realm of naked flesh. But in her questioning he cannot tell her it is the prostate. Such a confession would surely diminish all desire and reduce their conversation to something clinical and hospitalised. So he tries to joke.

He says, 'Sometimes I have trouble with my left foot. A collapsed arch. I wish I could make my left foot right.'

She laughs. 'Ha, you have some humour, old man.'

'I walk barefooted on the sand. You may have noticed.'

'Yes, I have noticed.'

'It is no worse. Nature may have intended us to be discalced like Brother Marías himself used to go about. Maybe there was method in it when I used to feel sorry for those Capuchins, thinking of chilblains as they paraded about Dublin in wintry weather.'

'You are homesick.'

'Nostos homecoming algos pain.'

'Nostalgia.'

'You go back in time and sometimes in pain not always but sometimes with jumps of joy or smarts of recognition and the accursed gaps like crosswords filling in spaces.'

The genitals grow and then shrivel. All the parts in repose. To awaken her dormant breasts, to feel their excitement reaching out to him. And her bare sallow arm tingling with hundreds of miniscule downy hairs, a little golden forest awaiting exploration.

This male gaze painted by a male hand and he wonders, How to ungender me.

The right and the wrong way. Is there such a thing? Desire is want, not need. The perspiration not from the heat but from the intensity of the desire hearing the siren's song —Calypso promising eternal youth— he wants to reach out to her, to touch her, to consume her, to be consumed by her, to be annihilated. To cease upon the midnight in ecstasy. But it is too much, even desire cannot grant all that. You are calling on a deity, not an impulse. The price of the two ways: putting back that shrivelled skin returning to that unfulfilled ageing creature who never really lived, whose life was a sublimation for some celestial utopia, a vacuous reward.

The second way: to fuck it all, delight in the expletive to fuck everything, all ethics and morals, all those shields so-called, cast aside. What good were they? At least say you have lived, you have justified a life not god-given but biologically-given even if it means, as she is hinting at all along, committing some nefarious deed.

To create something different other than those kitsch images religiously issued on factory conveyor belts. The image on the wall of his room placed by the Brother Superior after he was reprimanded and impressed on him that his own sketches and drawings, for what they were, were aberrational and demonstrated a weakness inherent in him and 'we all have weaknesses, Paul, and we have to guard against such weaknesses,' he says, like a stutter or Brother Marías' lisp.' It was something he had scarcely noticed, that needed to be overcome, so Brother Superior personally hammered with the nail an image that was meant to be uplifting, the bleeding heart of Christ, like no heart he had ever witnessed, to keep thoughts, especially at night, pure. Brother Superior whispered in his ear. 'Remember Paul, He is always looking down on us. He sees everything; nothing escapes him. Even in the dark.'

***

Maribel hears the voices in the adjoining room. Her mother's and some man's, not her father's. Another of her mother's lovers?

No, it is not a Latin voice. She remembers now it is the painter fellow, the old guy with the white beard; that's who it is, for she had heard his voice before talking to her mother. She knows what they are doing despite the bandages on her eyes. She had heard her mother offering to pose for him in return for saving her daughter. Her mother posing for that old guy. Her mother is a *libertina*. Maribel knows; she senses it in her bones that her mother is out there naked sitting before him for his titillation, or maybe as much hers as his, for her mother was always free with her body like that, not afraid to show it off. Her own mother behaving like this. She hears the voices and hears the easel moving, being adjusted. Could she not have repaid him, if that is the word, in some other way for saving her daughter's life? But he only did half the job. This guy saved half a life and he is being rewarded and hyped in the media as a hero which the nurse told her about, believing it was a great thing.

But how did he die, her Angelo? She asked Conchita. She was never told exactly just that he died, asphyxiated by the smoke. How sudden. He did not cry out. His heart just stopped when he was at the climax of his love with me. His heart literally broke, so he died of a broken heart. She was cross with him when he did not come that night, and Conchita immediately sprang to the boy's defence. After all he was from the same village as her. He was just a poor boy with his father dead, and it was not his fault that he could not come that night. His uncle needed him. She knows that now, how well she knows it when he said he had to go with his uncle. She was all dressed ready for him, but then he explained and he called to the villa, but she would not see him. And he told her later how he walked down the street jutting in and out of smoke screens looking for her, judging by the way his head and eyes were in constant swivel for anyone to see as Conchita explained searching *bocacalles* with a cough and a black fleck on his cheek. He saw her later from inside the window of *La Cuchara* and his eyes brightened. He entered, his white shirt dotted with carbon specks. He searched the tables but she was still cross with him and had gone to a bathroom until he had left crestfallen, walking out into the smoke filled street.

But the second night, oh he did come. And he was smiling and they held hands as they tripped along the cinder path oblivious to everything other than each other heading up the steep incline towards the mountain.

Was it her? Had she excited him too much in her flirtatious behaviour? For he could not wait to join with her, he was so carried away in his swoon that he did not see the world burning around him. And she too paid little attention to it, as they lay, feeling the flames were far away and would not reach them. All her fault, for it was she who led him on. Oh yes and she heard those old village women whispering their insinuations. But a boy so young overcome by the smoke more so than the flames. He was falling asleep, she remembers, from smoking the weed and the exhaustion of making love. How he exerted himself. '*Sí, mi cariña*,' Conchita says, 'he had a weak heart, and her voice trembles. 'I know that now,' Maribel says flicking a lock of hair away, 'but he had a strong heart for me, and I welcomed him into my very core to dwell there and never never leave. and we thought the heat was coming from our bodies.' And afterwards she tried to nudge him gently, for she was uncomfortable, but there was no move from him, and she could not bring herself to push him off after such ecstasy.

And she hears her mother's voice out there in the adjoining room. Is it a laugh? Surely she is not laughing. Maribel shouts out and rises from her bed and, with her white stick, bangs at the door of the debauched. 'Afuera,' she shouts bursting through the door, 'get away you base people. How can you, Mother, behave like this when there is death all around you? You are with him. I know you are with him. You have a man in Papá's bed. 'Go, get out,' and she strikes the air with her stick. 'Maribel,' Conchita calls. 'No no,' Maribel counters and she stumbles, and in so doing knocks down the easel.

13

They spend more time outdoors after Maribel's outburst especially by the ocean with the waves drowning out human voices as they crash on the shore. Viviana appears more relaxed now with no 'urgent' appointment no secret trysts especially with Maribel 'out of her hair' as she cruelly asserts back with her father in Madrid. 'Let him look after her for a while. They dote on each other you know. Let the Madrid doctors do what they can.'

The rocky coastline she prefers to the sandy beaches swarming with tourists and sunbathers. One or two bathers point at her in recognition as she removes her sunglasses to apply sun cream. He watches from under his wide straw hat which Viviana had purchased for him as she swims taking in her curves ebbing and flowing like waves, like the desire and the non-desire, and he is fearful that it could ebb away never to return. And he knows then what should be the beginning for him would be the end, for it is the life force, the spunk that propels. And he wonders how she seems so content almost to spend such an amount of time with him when she could be with this movie guy who promises her so much.

'Why don't you join me?' Her voice is distant like a seagull's.

'I can't swim.'

'Come in and I will teach you.'

'I am happy,' he says evening out the sand under him, 'just to watch you for the moment anyway.'

She dives as if to catch a fish like a wading bird and the seat of her bikini faces upwards causing an erection in him.

'It does something to one's well being,' she says as she surfaces and shakes out her hair matted from the brine'

'The ions.'

'Yes. Oh, look at the cheeky wave,' she shouts as a high wave nearly knocks her over. She regains her breath.

'Are you okay?' he says wading into the water and reaching out to steady her.

'The waves,' she says regaining her breath, 'are my friends. Except for that big wave, you see it, Pablo, overpowering me, my enemy wave.'

When she settles on her towel, noticing his erection, she says, 'How funny it is that the male body always betrays itself.'

'Yes,' he says shifting to adjust his shorts. 'We men have nowhere to hide, unlike women, in such matters.'

'*Such matters,*' she says stretching languorously. 'Oh Paul, do you know what a woman is? Is she the wave crashing in your mind?'

'Nothing as harsh as that,' he says with the salt spray licking at his lips. 'Maybe she is a quiet lake or the sky where it is not tormented.'

'Is that what you think, Paul? You think a woman is some static thing? You think there can be no storm in her life? Woman is torment, let me tell you.'

***

Walking along the coast distancing themselves from town and village, they discover a nudist beach.

'Spain is a country of many contrasts. You are learning,' she says seeing his jaw drop in unconcealed amazement at all the naked bodies lounging about. 'If you were in Galicia you could be arrested for taking your shirt off.'

'That was in Franco's time,' he says.

'The residue remains,'

'Weather and dark morals.'

'Ha.'

He proceeds to disrobe, disregarding his sunburn, wanting to feel that wonderful exultation of liberation that this is it, a serendipity, what is in his mind now, shedding not only his clothes but all the cloistered appendages that had cluttered and weighed down his previous existence. How come the body lets you down when the mind soars? His stomach is at him. Was it the smoked salmon or the bread, too fresh he had for lunch in that beachside restaurant?

'We are human above and fish below,' he says. 'Our origins are by the sea.'

'So I'm a mermaid now am I, in your scheme of things?'

'A slippery one.'

'Ha.'

She appears as she disrobes as free and easy as the birds in their shrill cries swooping over the waves. She thinks it is a great joke as she laughs at him struggling to get out of his shorts, and he unbalancing, nearly falling over in the sand.

But he can't do it. Not here in public. An invisible chain around him refuses to loosen.

'What is it, Pablo?' she says noticing his hesitation. 'You did it before.'

'I... I...,' he stammers with his clothes not quite knowing what to do with them. The floral shirt he folds and the pants linger with his hands akimbo looking around him like a little boy lost.

They eventually wind up sitting on sunbeds rented from a woman in a flowing dress and top and full of business with her money satchel strapped to her shoulder. They observe the naturists with Viviana's irreverent running comments about a rather pompous looking man with a tiny penis and his wife or partner, a middle-aged woman with enormous buttocks. 'There's your desire,' she whispers mockingly

Viviana has shed her beach robe and bikini effortlessly. She is naked except for her sunglasses, her disguise, no one recognising the famous actress as yet, no one caring, everyone too busy with their own little bumps and wobbles.

'What are you staring at?'

And she has generated a blush in Paul as he averts his gaze from the slight curls of her pubic hair.

'Are you not afraid?'

'Afraid of what? Por dios.'

'That photographer who—'

'Not here. What photographer could speed away on sand?' And she glares at him. 'Oh for god sake, Paul, are you going to take off those pants or not? Do you think your little monkey is something the world has never beheld?'

'It's not for everyone, is it, to behold I mean?'

'What does that mean?'

'It means... I don't know exactly. Perhaps...' and he thinks of Maribel, 'what I'm saying is it is not meant for everyone's gaze. Only for the one who— '

'What one?' She sounds exasperated, bored. Could she be bored, looking around her as if everything was normal?

'I don't know,' he says. 'I'm talking rubbish.'

'Ha. You are. What a prude you are. The prudish artist. It is a contradiction. You are afraid of your own nakedness and yet you want to expose mine for the world to see. Ha.'

But he cannot, no matter how hard he tries, his hands will not function to perform the task.

He sits on the sunbed still in his shorts and watches all the lolling bodies in their various shapes of nudity at play or swim or simply reclining under the strong rays of the sun. Paul begins to analyse what is wrong. Everything is too open, too in-your-face almost literally as a couple brushes past him on their way to the water. And he sees breasts that could succour a child on a stout reclining woman like two fried eggs sizzling in their oil. The very nature of desire is being usurped by these brazen creatures who refuse to cover themselves even in the beach café some metres away, shamelessly glued to the plastic seats flaunting themselves about as they drink and eat, challenging you if you catch their bold stares. Don't dare criticise, don't you dare attempt to introduce a moral theme here.

'Bums are just bums in this place,' he concludes after an hour or so when she questions him about why he wishes to leave.

He longs to return to the rocks, the quiet secluded place, as something offering camouflage and some privacy to allow desire to grow again. The place of the naked no longer interests him.

Viviana shrugs. 'Whatever,' she says and she slips into her bathrobe and catches her beach bag up on her shoulder.

'You have not managed it yet.'

'What?'

'And somehow I don't think you ever will.'

'What for god sake?'

'To realise that nakedness is conquest over inhibition.'

'But you know Vivianna, it is my very inhibitions that enhance the eroticism. If I lose that, bad and all as it is, I will also lose as a corollary...'

'As a corollary? *Por dios.*'

'...the eroticism. It will be just reduced to those naked dangling bits we witnessed on the beach.'

And, perhaps still feeling that he will be of use to her, she follows him to endure the inconvenience of the kilometre walk to the rocky shore in the searing afternoon sun.

And even to see two corpulent naked men walking along the footpath away from the beach as if they are trying to make a statement, merely makes them look awkward, he thinks, as they negotiate the asphalt, and whatever about in the context of the sea here on the open road with buses and traffic passing, they, with their exposed wobbly bits, look absurd. Or perhaps it is the concrete world that is out of place. Perhaps if they were among jungle vegetation, but even then Tarzan wore a loincloth. But that was just Hollywood.

'I thought you found it liberating,' she says, noticing his unease, 'all this.'

'You know that painting by Manet about the naked woman in the company of the two clothed men?'

'*Le Déjeuner sur l'hierbe.*'

'Yes. Well I felt like the woman. I felt naked, but I felt the others were clothed.'

'You felt the nudists were clothed.' She laughs.

'Yes and I was not the one who gazed but rather the subject of the gaze.'

'Oh Paul, what has that Congregation done to you? Don't you know, you the artist, that the naked body is only a point of departure for the work of art?'

'You know so much.'

'No, everybody knows that and I am surprised at you not knowing it. Will we get a taxi?'

'You said Paul. Again,' he says ignoring her question.

'I did, and that is all you take note of. You told me you liked Velázquez.'

'But not only for his art, but also for his contradiction.'

'Meaning?'

'Perhaps it's like the ying and yang in my own mind.'

'What on earth are you talking about?'

'I can identify with Velázquez because he is a painter who seemed to have been able to live within the contradiction inside himself.'

'Everyone has contradictions.'

No, I mean in the extreme. Like how on the one hand can he paint the glorious *Immaculate Conception* for example and on the other *Venus at her toilet, naked.*

'His wife was the model for the Virgin,' she says, 'and as regards the other, don't you know all those nudes were the soft porn of the their time to titillate the aristocracy, the moneyed class, those who could afford to offer patronage for such indulgences. *La maja desnuda,* which you previously referenced had a dreadful face. Manet's *Olympia* would be a more worthy exemplum or perhaps Velasquez's *Rokeby Venus*, far more sensuous than Manet, don't you think?'

'You know your art.'

'Oh Paul, art is just a manifestation of lust. How can you be such a simpleton?'

'No, not a simpleton, maybe just naïve with little experience of the world.'

'Of course.'

'So now I know,' he says feigning hurt, 'you use Paul when you want to pillory me. Paul the sinner.'

'You think that?'

'The soul is form and doth the body make.'

'Is that a quote?'

'From Spenser.'

'You have forgotten I don't believe in the soul.'

'I was thinking of that, of what you said.'

'And your conclusion?'

'If you don't believe in the soul that means by way of corollary that you don't believe in conscience. I mean a moral conscience.'

'Conscience just makes cowards of us, you know your Shakespeare, Pablo. So,' she seems smug, the look of confidence, 'who wants such a thing if it means being a coward?' She regards him challengingly. 'You are not a coward, Pablo? The way you entered that burning forest.'

'That was bravado,' he says, and afterwards he thinks, maybe she is right in her interpretation—conscience really does make cowards of us all.

14

He is early when he arrives at her villa, ten minutes or so before eleven, the designated hour. Viviana has not yet risen. He is concerned about Maribel. The manner of her outburst. Conchita lets him in and he declines her offer of tea seeing she has enough to do with her arms full of towels and crumpled sheets. He will wait for Viviana by the pool where the early sun glistens over the blue water endowing the chemical chlorine a false orthodoxy. He is sitting on a wicker chair, his easel and cotton bag placed by his side, when he hears a rooting sound. He looks up and sees Maribel in dark glasses coming through the French door. Viviana had not told him she had returned from Madrid. She is rooting with her stick which becomes stuck among the flower beds. He rises and goes to her.

'Can I help you?'

She stops and cocks her ear. She is dressed in a white linen dress, her feet bare in cork sandals.

'I am Paul Guilfoyle, the man who—'

'You,' she says, 'you want to help me?' The voice sounds so much older than her years.

'I thought if I can direct you to a chair perhaps.' There were three other wicker chairs around the pool and a sunbed. 'Would you like to sit in the sun? It is nice now, the morning not too hot.'

'You want to help me.' She laughs. He realises now the repetition is not a question but a mockery, an accusation, and the tone reminiscent of her mother.

'You, *forastero,* came to our country and helped me before, remember? You saw what good that did. Maybe it is good that you should help me again. I could lose something else, a leg or an ear perhaps.'

'Maribel, I am very sorry for what happened. Please sit down. Let us talk. Your condition I have heard the doctors say may be reversed.'

'Ha,' she says, 'some chance of that with the lacerations they performed on me.'

'I understand it must be very difficult for you. But there is hope, Maribel. We must be patient.'

'Who are you to tell me to be patient? Has my mother been talking? She hears voices you know talking to herself again. She thinks she's famous. Has she told you she is a famous film star? It is all made up. It's all in her head, all wishful thinking.'

'But the newspapers, they—'

'Ha, the newspapers. They just like taking photographs. They think she is great because she appeared in some local films in the past. A big fish you know in shallow water.'

'But the Italian producer, surely— '

'Ha, another of her lovers she seduced to get a part. You know that's the way my mother operates. She seduces men to get something for herself.'

She tilts her head towards Paul. 'And you señor, has she seduced you yet? What does she want to get out of you I wonder. You are a painter by all accounts. Are you going to satisfy her vanity with a portrait? Do you really think that will be enough to satisfy her? She is never satisfied. That is the problem with her.'

She cocks her head once more and sniffs the air, as if she is searching for something, her pert nose more pointed than her mother's.

'Do you know I asked my mother once if she loved me. She said what is love? When I wanted to talk to her she switched the subject to some utterings from dead philosophers. Can you believe it? What can I do with my mother? She is my mother, you know.'

'I know. Maribel, can I—?'

'I think the air is foul here,' she says and she turns and goes back towards the house with her stick tapping to find the step. 'Papá,' she shouts, 'where is Papá? I want to go home.'

Viviana does not appear. She sends Conchita to inform him she is not feeling well, and Paul wonders is it to do with her daughter's return. He leaves, thinking of Maribel's surgeons and lives lost and saved by man's intervention. And his mind wanders back to San Salvador: the tumult, the frenzy that followed those murders when all order broke down and the secret he kept all those years. The streets were wild with soldiers firing indiscriminately, people screaming, the smell of gunpowder, explosions blinding one's vision, the looting, the pinning up against a wall and the shooting, the raping. Paul was trying to make his way back to the monastery several streets away. He had been to visit a wounded Irish Brother caught in the gunfire who was taken in by nuns into their convent. He was to arrange for his return to the monastery to his own Brotherhood, but the Spanish-speaking nuns said the wounded Brother was too weak to move. Perhaps in a few days. A stressed doctor was already tending the wound —a stray bullet that had just missed his heart.

The firing outside increased. He left the wounded man and turned into a side street trying to avoid some of the mayhem thinking it might be a shortcut. Up against an old crumbling wall of a dilapidated store house with mortar weeping down its side he saw a soldier with his khaki trousers around his ankles. He was holding a bayonet against a young woman's throat as he proceeded to rape her. Paul could make out the dark terrified eyes of the woman over the soldier's shoulder as she cried out in anguish calling to Paul. She was directing her eyes towards him as the soldier thrust into her and, mistaking Paul for a priest because of his dog collar, she shouted '*Por favor padre, ayúdame.*' Blood trickled from her neck. '*Cállese puta,*' the soldier snarled. Paul was convinced that, as the bayonet plunged deeper, the soldier would kill the woman when he had satisfied his urge. The deeper he thrust the more the blood pumped out of her. A strength took hold of Paul then. He was convinced it was the spirit of the Holy Ghost entering him as he hoisted the soldier off the woman. The soldier, struggling and cursing, tried to stab Paul with his bayonet. But he was just a small, skinny fellow with a black pencil moustache, and Paul grabbed his wrist and twisted his arm inwards forcing the point of the bayonet into his entrails. The soldier slumped down in a pool of his own blood and the girl, holding her neck, ran away into the darkness.

Paul moved quickly down the side street as he heard rough voices approaching, but he did not run, he did not want to draw attention to himself. He found his way back to the monastery and told his superior about the sick Brother and then excused himself to his room. He kept to himself for several days after that and never told anyone of his experience—that he had killed a man, he was convinced. There was blood on his hands which he had hidden from his superior. He looked at them, strong, thick-fingered and milky white. What strange organs that can do such a deed. He remembers scrubbing them under the hot tap with soap and nailbrush, each individual finger, each accomplice in the act he scrubbed preparedly, the black red congealing blood of another man, a mother's son, a husband, a father perhaps, Paul had taken his life away. No matter what he was doing to the girl, had he the right...? He agonised on it in sleepless nights wishing Brother Marías was with him at that moment. He surely would have counselled him. For days he wandered where there were no roads, just dirt tracks that twisted and curved and seemed to go nowhere in keeping with the wild ramifications of his mind. What had he done? Who could he speak to? Who was there to know he had broken The Third Commandment?

Then after about a week, when the gun fire in the streets abated, he made a rational decision to put what he had done to the back of his mind. The wounded Brother eventually returned to the monastery and made a complete recovery. The bayoneted girl he never saw again.

15

'I was too bright to be a mere starlet of the casting couch, my father said, for their bright lights, no substance— a favourite phrase of his— you are a woman of substance. He insisted that I continue my studies. He wanted to shape me into some culture vulture, a scion of himself, his only child. But I wanted more. I suppose I wanted it all in fact, all that the world had to offer, the glitter and the intellect. I did not see any dichotomy in combining both qualities of looks and brains.'

And Paul thinks, how vain to say she is beautiful and brainy too, but then who can dispute it? She seems relaxed, the medication working, the doctor is leaving through the open door as Paul arrives with just the curt non-eye contact *Buenos días*.

He would love to accost this doctor, this small weedy looking man with his bag of tricks in his leather briefcase, stop him in his headlong tracks to ask him exactly why he is attending Viviana, what she is suffering from and what he is prescribing. Can the medication have something to do with her mood swings and occasional rants or are those traits intrinsic to her? But Paul knows as a mere stranger he is unlikely to be given any answers by this doctor, who undoubtedly would claim, like a priest in confession, medical confidentiality.

All he can muster to Viviana is, 'I see the doctor visited.'

'He knows nothing,' she says. 'All he does is take his fee and leave.'

'Doctor No Fuss.'

She smiles. 'Don't be too nosey, señor. Doctors come and go like summer breezes. Sometimes the breeze is gentle and other times ...well you know...'

'I was talking to Maribel,' he says.

'And what?'

'She says you were never a great star,' he says, deciding to make a clean breast of it to gauge her reaction and to try to get to the truth. 'That it's all in your head.'

'Liars all,' she fumes. 'Everyone is a liar, saying such a thing, *la cerda*, about me her mother. Take your pick, Paul, which liar do you prefer?'

'Forgive me,' he says amazed at his own forthrightness, but his work is paramount and he is fearful she could dismiss him again as she did previously when the mood seized her.

'Let me tell you,' she says calming down, 'the way it was. They told me I had the looks, the dark sultry looks of the Latina as they called me. But the brains they seemed to miss out on. I had just graduated from university and my head was full of all sorts of philosophy and rant imposed by the likes of you Paul with your theology. I wanted to shake off that work to taste the glitter, to hell with my father, I was twenty-three for god sake and when an audition came up for an American-produced film in Almería—the Americans liked the sun and the near desert conditions for their spaghetti westerns— I became the glamour bit of a big rancher. It was vanity of course to be admired and gazed upon and even lusted after by half the world as I appeared in my skimpy outfits and a couple of not-so-subtle nude flashes like the skirt riding up as I was abducted by the Apaches in one of the B-movies. It was a start for what I really wanted, the role of a femme fatale where there was real meat, something I could really get my teeth into.'

'Are you one of those women,' he says, 'I mean in real life, Viviana, are you a femme fatale?'

'Femmes fatales are fiction, Paul don't you know that?'

'Of course,' he says.

'In my imagination I had illusions like you with your fantasies about desire. Even as a teenager having seen many film noirs, most of them dubbed alas but nevertheless I would dream of this power femmes fatales had and what they could do with that power.' She sighs. 'But of course the reality was the opposite.'

'Which was?'

'Javier would never leave me alone. He'd be always phoning or texting, delighted that I was working here in *la patria*—Oh a patriotic fellow is our Javier— and not in some foreign land, always claiming he was worried about me, yes *muy preocupado*. I had no peace, and he would come to see me filming on the set asserting to the hard-pressed officials he had a government brief to promote the industry.'

'He was actually promoting your film?'

You see, there was a lot of isolationism after the civil war. A lot of countries did not want to fraternise with Franco after his association with Hitler and the savagery of his dictatorial methods, but he wanted to woo people to his country. He wanted American dollars, that was Spanish foreign policy for a while and it worked to give American strategic bases in Spain to encourage tourism and where I came in.'

'You?'

'Yes, he wanted me to encourage those Hollywood moguls to make their spaghetti westerns in the deserts of southern Spain.'

'So, he was happy as long as—'

'I didn't roam yes. Once I was here at home in the *patria* things were fine. It suited his purpose. He wasn't a minister then you know.'

'So, you were instrumental in—'

'He doesn't acknowledge it of course but yes, the kudos all fell into his lap. However, once he had that prestigious position, that power in the limelight, which is what he craved for himself in the only way he knew how... he wanted me back as his chattel or rather the glossy side of himself.'

'To show off.'

'Yes. I was his trophy, but what do you do with a trophy?'

'And Maribel?'

'Yes Maribel, the interjection in the affair. And I thought of my father's words extolling the intellect and so I was carried away with an emotion far superior. I was to be the feted wife of the new minister for the environment, appointed by the king no less. The childhood sweetheart had come good.'

'Whom you used to taunt.'

'It wasn't just me, you know. It was through his father's influence, a lackey of Franco that he got into politics, a man of bad blood which obviously runs in the veins of his children.'

She sits at the glass-topped wrought iron table by the pool and calls for Conchita to bring them coffee.

'You know although my father was a very educated man, he was incapable of expressing a basic emotion. I always tried to please him in the hope that he would say something nice to me. That's why I excelled in exams because that would make him happy, but he never expressed anything. He never expressed that pleasure. So maybe that's why I sought that pleasure in other ways.' She looks at him. 'Do you see?'

'Is that why you are like that too, towards Maribel I mean...?'

'I am not like that,' she says dismissively. 'But my father was so learned. Older men Paul, can have great wisdom, and when I look at you I think of my father and wisdom. You Pablo, are special. You have wisdom and other things besides.'

'You flatter me,' he says. 'And what other things would I have?'

'Well, you are an artist which is a wonderful thing and...'

'Yes.'

'You're sexy, Paul. Older men can be sexy and...'

'And?'

'Vain,' she says. 'You are fishing for compliments. But you have all this stuff in you that has never been released. I can help you. We can both help each other escape from the prison of ourselves.'

'And where does your husband fit into all of this?'

'Oh Javier.' She tuts. 'Despite being a government minister, he is just a fatuous creature. He knows nothing of the world. Javier is up in arms if I so much as look at another man. But as for me now,' she says blinking her Cleopatra eyelashes, 'I prefer a man with greying hairs, a sign of maturity. Maturity is sexy, don't you think?'

'Am I really to believe that? What about this Benito fellow?'

'That's business,' she says sharply.

There is a moment of silence as Conchita arrives and places the tray with the coffee cups and silver pot down on the table.

'Go,' she snaps at Conchita who looks over at Paul almost pleadingly he thinks before she withdraws through the French doors.

'Why are you always so curt to her?'

'You think I am curt? Give them an inch Paul and they will cut your throat.'

'How can you say that?'

'Believe me, I know those Andalusian gypsies. They resent any wealth in others. They carry deep resentment going back to the *latifundios*. They simmer inside, so they have to be kept in their place.'

'But is she not from the same village as you?'

'Oh she is from there now all right. But she was not always from there. She was born in a caravan. Her people came from caravans.'

***

It was the gangster movies taking her out of her comfort zone, out of the predictable desert spaghetti films which were made in Spain and which she could now make in her sleep. She would have to go to Hollywood. But this new venture was a challenge, was more noir. She dreamed she would have a white telephone and sleep between satin sheets. At least that is what she thought, not taking into account that it would be mainly Javier who would ring her on it apart of course from the seedy producers who would want to know if they could come up to her room. An older cousin had moved to Hollywood. She had married an architect who made a fortune designing houses for the film stars. She invited Viviana, if she were to come over, to stay with them at their villa where she could breakfast in the early morning sun in its everlastingness in her bikini at their giant heart-shaped swimming pool with their sunbeds and palm trees and high surrounding laurel hedges.

She was to play a gangster's moll all sultry and steamy looks and tight gowns and lingering glimpse of exposed thigh, all that was par for the course, but this time when she examined the script there was better dialogue, she was allowed to be witty and caustic like Marlene Dietrich whom she admired. She liked being caustic. She was capable of extemporising and adlibbing like some of the big-named actors who never followed a script and got away with it. She was even invited eventually when she met the Italian producer Benito Fudoli to be codirector so that she would have a say, not only in her own acting but in the whole production. It was a dream come true and everything was arranged by Benito. But Javier would not let her go. She had already auditioned before she got married but had heard nothing and presumed she did not get the part. The delay was due to difficulty in funding and it took over a year for her to be informed that the film was going ahead and she had got the part. It was a major boost to her career to advance from the previous wooden roles she had to act out. She was to star opposite a top male Hollywood actor, his name only waiting to be confirmed. But Javier wouldn't let her go. She was planning on ignoring him, of going it alone, she tells Paul, but then she got ill, didn't she? She had one of her turns. And Javier was all caring for her and making her feel homesick. 'Don't want you going to that place You'll be treated as a *puta*. No wife of mine will be treated like that.' And he was thinking at the time of his reputation in the Cortes. 'You will bring shame to me and our country.'

She breathes in deeply and exhales. 'So you see, Pablo, I succumbed. I was lonely. I was mixed up, unsure of myself and he was a pillow, an easy pillow to lie on, but I didn't realise in time that same pillow would suffocate me.'

16

'You are there,' she says sensing him as she comes out tapping with her stick touching the grooves between the tiles. 'I can hear a rat rustling.'

Paul is sitting on the wicker chair trying to be inconspicuous, not to move or scrape the chair off the tile and leaving his easel in freeze frame. He was always like that in the Congregation, trying to be far enough away not to draw attention to himself; the man who would blush whenever he had to address a group except, and he reflected, when he was dealing with the poor or talking in Spanish. In Spanish he had a new-found confidence.

'Why do you allow that rat, Mother, scurry about on our property?'

'You are alive, be thankful,' Viviana says coming through the French door.

'I don't want to be alive.'

'Don't say such things. You are only sixteen. You have life ahead of you.'

'How could it happen?' she cries out. 'How could Angelo be dead? I loved him, Mother.'

'You hardly knew him, child.'

And so they continue, the arguments between mother and daughter. What can one say to a blind person who feels so maligned? A young girl on the cusp reduced to what now he cannot say, that the subject of his desire is dependent on the sense of sight? What she witnessed when she beheld her Angelo, if that is taken away like Samson or Milton would he then be relieved, that itch of the flesh fanned by the eye, an onus, an urge removed, one less in the tedious advancement of life? Would the subject of his desire be requited by being thus nullified? And Maribel, on learning of her state, what torments she must suffer. If she had not been whetted, if the flame had been ignited in her a year or two earlier, if it had happened then, that affliction at a prepuberty stage, would her cry have been as shrill?

***

The first time she drew him towards her physically was indoors when the nose was causing frustration after several attempts with pencil and charcoal, the blemishes of which Brother Marías had shown him how to erase with stale bread.

'Your shorts are wet. You pee'd on them.'

'It was just tap water splashing,' he lies. 'When I was washing the brushes.'

'Come here to me Pablo,' she says, 'and throw away that dog's crust.'

The fan is whirring and she is reclining on the chaise longue with only the bathrobe hanging loosely from her shoulders. 'You need a break. I see life's thwarting in your eyes. I know men and their needs. Come.'

He puts away his pencils and goes towards her feeling awkward being summoned to the real world from his artistic bubble. Like Adam coming out of the garden perhaps or maybe coming into the garden for her arms are drawing him on seductively.

'There is great heat today.'

The thought: Helios can overpower us or set us free.

We must buy a second fan. That one is useless. Come sit by my side.'

'Maribel?'

'She is sleeping.'

Viviana flips onto her belly. 'I am not forgetting,' she says, 'the way you like to ogle me.'

'Hardly ogling,' he says, 'more admiring.'

'No need to worry. I'm used to that, men's stares and of course always with can't-keep-his-hands to himself Javier tormenting me. That was when we were younger. Now his actions are more measured, since he became a minister, the hand on my bottom in public now a thing of the past. But I am no longer interested in his hands or any other part of him for that matter, his mauling. No woman likes to be mauled. A woman, Pablo, needs to be caressed... so now you can look at me up close but not as an artist or some celibate monk, but as a man of *carne y hueso*.'

The heat is fierce despite the second fan, and beads of sweat are flowing down her breast and even the modest Paul has removed his shirt. Why, despite her affluence, he wonders, has she not invested in air conditioning?

She stops suddenly as if only now realising her surrounding and looks at him.

'Are you hot?'

'Well...' He hesitates expecting her to offer some solution.

'I'm hot. Very hot, Pablo.'

17

It was Brother Marías who taught him Spanish together with two of the other young postulants who volunteered and could be sent to sister houses in South America. It was almost like a hobby with Brother Marías, casual and laid back in his room on Saturday mornings with Paul and three or four of his fellow students still in their teens. He taught them from his Hills and Ford grammar and consulted his old, tattered Cuya's dictionary which he had brought from Spain wherever there was a semantic difficulty. The grammar book Brother Marías had bought in the second hand section of Greens old book shop on Nassau Street. He told Paul he was the custodian of books and he would be sent into town every autumn to purchase religious books with an inventory dictated by the Brother Superior: books on meditation mainly and Catholic dogma. It was on one of those trips he also purchased on his own initiative the heavy tome of religious paintings which he kept in his room rather than in the library of the monastery. The Brother Superior never noticed the additional purchase. But from the Hills and Ford book Paul learned the rudiments of Spanish grammar and Brother Marías was not withdrawn then but happy in talking about his home place, the old Moorish village of A—, and he expounded on Arabs and Christians, but not in the confrontational ways Paul was used to hearing in his church history lessons. They lived side by side with us, Brother Marías said, in the village which was originally theirs. *Vecinos*. They were our neighbours. He elaborated about his homeland and all varied aspects of that great Iberian peninsula. The people of Spain north and south were chalk and cheese like sun and rain in extremes of conviction. And Brother Marías talked about the civil war and conflicting ideologies that drove people to kill. He never said which side he was on and Paul often wondered later if it was possibly the republican side, and that may have been a doubt that tormented him, for he never spoke of the

Church in triumphalist terms but as a place for Jesus and children and innocence and charity. Suffer the little children to come unto you was a favourite saying of his and he often quoted the parable of the loaves and fishes and the little local boy offering his food to Jesus in faith, and Jesus multiplied them for the thousands of hungry who came to listen to him. Faith was the thing that moved mountains, not armies or tyrannies; they were the opposite thing, the contrarian thing to the life of Jesus and his beloved Saint Thomas à Kempis—*The Imitation of Christ* was on his bedside locker. Brother Marías hated the Crusades. How can you carry a cross and sword in the same hands? The grammar he loved, the discipline it provided; all of life should be contained within a grammar so that we can parse ourselves, so that we never need to worry about uncertainty. Spanish derived from the Latin, has a wonderful logic. But when he came to the saints there was a contradiction in himself, for their mysticism destroyed all the constructs and gave language a new dimension, a power to reach out to god, and that was Brother Marías' ultimate aim. Language is a key, he said, a tool to help us to find a path, a stairway yes — he used that word quite often— to the Creator, and when we reach that height we will feel ecstasy, but only a few, only very few ever reach those heights. And Paul felt such overpowering emotions emanating from Brother Marías that it was transported to himself and he could not wait for Saturday to arrive; it was the highlight of his week. Soon however, the other postulants quit the classes. He remembered one of them saying that Brother Marías was wandering off the mark and should focus more on the religious calling, particularly our role as teachers which he hardly mentioned, and they eventually dropped out of the class either tiring of the grammatical complexities of a foreign language — what was the subjunctive mood all about?— or due to Brother Marías' idiosyncratic way of teaching. But Brother Marías didn't seem to mind as long as Paul persevered, which he did alone, for Paul was beginning to love Brother Marías.

They were teaching Brothers in South America. He considered originally opting for Africa on the basis of an uncle, his mother's brother, a priest who had experience there. But he was sent to one of their houses in San Salvador because he had some Spanish. He had taken classes in the seminary of All Hallows in Drumcondra with its creaky oak floors and smell of mould and where some of his fellow postulants (mainly for priesthood) were bound for Mexico. He was a missionary Brother after all, although his previous years were spent teaching in a north Dublin school where the sound of pupil-teacher arguments and physical punishment and detentions constituted most of the activity among the staff including lay teachers who were considered, to his disapproval by the superiors, as a 'necessary evil' to fill the gap in religious numbers. His approach and indeed that of his mentor Brother Marías of softer spoken words did not succeed that well in classrooms of thirty plus boisterous boys. He was reading a lot even then about art and poetry and he found an increasing conflict in the more refined his sensibilities became from such reading and his day work, paralleling a corresponding diminution of interest for the most part in those whom he had the misfortune to teach. And he was glad when the call came in his twenty-fifth year to fill the vacancy on the death of an old Brother in the congregation house in San Salvador. He arrived there when the smoke bombs filled the streets during the funeral of the assassinated archbishop Romero. He saw the rifle shots from the buildings on the TV, the stampede, the forty odd people killed. Bring a sword or bring peace. More praxis less doctrine, that was the stage he was at then in his beliefs which were still strong at that time. He thought he could do something to help. The assassination of Romero moved him greatly. How cheap was life supposedly sacred, how easy to quench by these manipulators or bullets all the meaning, all the effort of one's life and one's sacrifices obliterated just like that in an instant whiff of smoke. He felt part of the persecuted Christ and of the people of the poor and the dispossessed and he thought of all the street urchins in Waterford long ago which the wealthy business man Ignatius Rice witnessed, moving him to action and the founding of a Christian Brotherhood to which he belonged. And he thought that life was all about transformation from rich to poor materially but a gaining of spiritual wealth. The word of God was mediated through the cries of the poor and the oppressed and he was His instrument. Indeed, in some quarters the people thought God was Irish because of all the Irish names associated with the dissemination of the Catholic faith there. To have from the bottom up a Christian-based community was the hope. But the bottom up took on such a totally different meaning here now like Goya, like the satanic guffaws, like the key to our base instincts: prostitutes were once virgins and saints were once sinners. That is a levelling thought. That was then. That's what he was like then. The early Christians suffered persecution by the established order. Why should it be different now? Suffering is the badge of all our tribe—these phrases that suffuse his brain from school-learned Shakespeare. So what is new in that? Except that we have gone away from it with the riches and the gold plundered from the colonised world, from which we built great cathedrals from the blood of vanquished peoples: Incas and Indians and blacks all for the glorification of the western god.

But he concentrated on the teaching as he was instructed to do. It was far easier in Latin America than in Dublin, and more basic. The pupils were pliant and poor and grateful, most of all grateful. The ease of that work gave him more time to concentrate on the burning social issues of street children, and he took on a juvenile prison ministry under the magnetism of Blessed Ignatius Rice, believing 'the good seed will grow up in the children's hearts'.

And he remembered: The seed wasted on the barren rock. The steel bed creaking in a darkness, the cries of the forsaken seeing Him, beseeching him for succour to forgive them for their sinfulness. But why? They did not ask for such apparel, to be so equipped the way they were, the rise and fall, was that sinful or a natural impulse, seeking a meaning, a life out of the darkness? What did it all signify? Weighed down by original sin, the weight of it for being born to carry such a load. The false taint, the fake news, all in hindsight now.

He always drew; it was in the monastery strangely enough where he honed this skill: two doves fighting on a branch, his first attempt accepted to illustrate a children's religious book— The Child Jesus in all his dreamy technicolour. But his doves were interpreted and indeed extolled, not as fighting, but as sharing the branch. The dove, the symbol, a shitting pigeon as he remembers him, for he did not wish to glamorise a pigeon as a dove in a halo of light but to present it as it really was. However, this drawing ability landed him in trouble on more than one occasion. He drew caricatures of Brother Banville, a stout bullying fellow making the drawing more real than exaggerated. For the caricature was in fact a fellow who liked to keep his Buddha-like belly well filled and had a permanent bag of toffee sweets concealed under his soutane. Paul was disciplined when it was discovered, the drawing doing the rounds of fellow postulants. He was told never to draw again and that, apart from the insult which he had delivered to the reverend Brother, what he was engaging in was really a vanity. So he needed to undertake a retreat and concentrate on higher values and not on the world of shadows, to withdraw from that material world full of corrupting influences and temptation. The drawing before it was destroyed at an auto-da-fe ceremony, was raised in the assembly hall as a symbol to demonstrate to other novices the error of his ways, and this of course dented any idea he may have had that his drawings were good. But he agonised about this in his bed in (in hindsight) the appropriately named Saint Augustine's dorm and lay awake listening to the ejaculatory sounds of some of his fellow students lost in a world of darkness which of course was always forgotten in the dawn after cold showers which is the antidote, the antonym, of biological urges.

So he agonised. He felt it was unfair, what he was being ordered to do. His drawings represented his way of perceiving the world after all, for it was not only caricatures he drew but the world of nature. He also tried to delineate particularly trees and birds before developing a preoccupation with the female form, and this he now realises was due initially to the excitability of its proscribed state and all his sublimations and his nescience of the opposite gender. So his attempted portrayal, which nearly led to his expulsion from the congregation, after a huge and long lasting brouhaha culminated instead in his banishment to their outer colonies when others more worldly remained and yet continued in their base ways. But an image was far worse than a base action; the image was something de facto, something constructed like the printed word and could exert a binding influence on some impressionable novice, already tainted.

What he was trying to do was to discover through the meandering of a Derwent pencil the essence of the female form and in so doing discover the essence of male desire itself. For if these drawings had not been discovered he would have left eventually anyway. It was the spur that drove him from the order, for he realised that by not drawing he was giving up his individual life, what he was, what he was meant to be without any impositions. Draped in unending sombre colours he became conscious that he was being sucked into an abyss. And that he was not prepared to do. And while his notion of a god diminished, that sense of a vocation increased, however no longer for religion but now transferred to the realm of art.

It was after the incident with the sketches and before the banning that Brother Marías showed Paul his book of religious paintings, and he remembers Rene's San Sebastian in ecstasy with the arrows piercing his side particularly appealed to the brother, and various paintings of the Madonna, and especially the Immaculate Conception by Velázquez, and the highly stylized works of el Greco.

'You can keep up your drawings,' he whispered into Paul's ear, 'no matter what they say.'

'It would be an act of disobedience.'

'You have talent, Paul. I have seen it. And you know what Jesus says about using your talents and not to bury them in the sand or deny them for that matter. So I have a suggestion for you on how to overcome the problem. Take this book. Copy all the religious paintings by the masters until you become proficient to do your own. They will not be able to object to that, for your act will be construed as part of the promulgation of the faith and would be lauded in fact.'

It was some years later before he learned that those religious painters also created secular images— images which did not appear in any of the pious books in the monastery, but Brother Marías kept them in a locked drawer in his bedside cabinet: large full page copies capturing the sumptuous colour of the originals which Paul was later to learn of in the Prado and other galleries.

Coloured vestments blackened by centuries of oil and candle smoke. How did they marry the two? He asked Brother Marías. God and Mammon, surely... but the word was made flesh, he said to Paul looking at him with shining angelic eyes like Jesus himself, and Paul thought of the film they had shown in the monastery that week called Marcelino about the young boy sacrificing his life to save the Eucharist which he was transporting to the Christians in the catacombs and which was hidden in his jerkin from the Roman soldier.

'Remember that film Paul, it was the most beautiful film ever, was it not?' 'Yes' said Paul, 'the word did become flesh. It cannot be denied what the Brother Superior is asking us to do.'

'Us?' Brother Marías kept his voice low and looked towards the door of his room for fear of being overheard. 'What they are asking us to do is to deny the flesh which is tantamount to denying Jesus. You understand? It can't be done. Santa Teresa for example was in love with an absent person. How can you love a vacuum? She was in perpetual wonder of her own mind. A mystic, a pioneer of the subconscious. And did you know the right hand of Santa Teresa was kept by Franco until his death, captured from republican troops during the civil war in Ronda?'

And he remembered the evening after one of the Spanish classes when he had made great linguistic strides, mastering the subjunctive mood, Brother Marías came towards him as Paul was about to go out the door and his eyes gazed on Paul and Paul thought they were going to burst out of their sockets such was their intensity. Brother Marías rested his palm on Paul's shoulder and said, 'You are Pablo, my special friend,' and then he cried.

When Paul went to South America they had maintained a correspondence, Brother Marías always writing on the familiar tiny squared notepaper which reminded him of Spain and the graph paper he used in school (he sometimes enclosed a John Hinde postcard of Ireland 'in case you are homesick'). He asked Paul if he still had the Robinia plant he had given him. He was gratified to hear that Paul still had the plant and was looking after it and carried it with him wherever he was sent. They communicated in Spanish. Paul looked forward to the weekly missive. Apart from improving his Spanish, it sustained him in his work no matter how wretched it was. It was wonderful to share each other's views on what a Christian life should be—what a real calling was—, what a vocation meant. 'Some are called,' Brother Marías wrote, 'because they can hold beating hearts in their hands.' But then as Paul was about to tell him of his killing of the soldier, the missives stopped.

It was a dull November day when Paul came home from the mission. There was a light drizzle and he wore a waterproof anorak with the hood up as he walked along the towpath of the meandering ribbon of the canal, and he remembers seeing a llama among the grazing sheep in a field looking forlorn, homesick.

His Spanish had become fluent and his Portuguese passable after wide travelling through the continent, his knowledge of the favelas and poor barrios of south America expert and highly sought after. He departed the mission house the Stella Maris college in Montevideo where he had toiled for several months doing mainly administrative work for the order: writing letters, communicating with home base in Ireland as his request has been granted by the Congregation to research the level of poverty and to conduct a report on the favelas with the possibility of the congregation opening a house in Brazil. The largest period of time he spent with any group was in the favelas. He had got special permission from the superior general to undertake research first-hand about the underclass, a term he hated, preferring to refer to the indigenous inhabitants as underprivileged and simply poor, but more than that they were people that could be any of us were it not for the grace of god. And the man he had killed haunted him for many sleepless nights.

He had made friends with some of the poor families and he returned to Ireland a confirmed socialist, but not a born-again Christian. He didn't like that tag: a number of the new activist priests and Brothers had tried to convert him to their radical ideology. We need to change things, it is no good just praying. We need to protest, they said, even if it does expose ourselves to the corrupt *juntas*. But how can you sit idly by and watch the rich prosper and the poor starve? The perennial problem that will never change, he is convinced of now.

During a thunder and lightning storm he remembers witnessing the destruction of many of the huts, the dwelling places of thousands of undernourished families. A particular affecting moment for him was when the floods and mudslides swept away a little baby from its mother's breast. Before his eyes he witnessed it, the force of the water tearing the baby from its mother's nipple and sweeping it along the current grimed in mud and slime and he tried to slide with it to reach out to save the baby, but he could not reach it and the baby was swept away.

Paul decided to call to the old monastery in Dublin on a grey afternoon to pay his respects to Brother Marías. Not having heard from him, he was anxious to enquire about his health. One of the old retired Brothers whom Paul vaguely recognised opened the heavy front door with the tall fanlight to admit him.

There was a hushed atmosphere among some of the Brothers who nodded to Paul. They were polite but slid along the corridor away from him with their hands up their sleeves like drifting ghosts. He waited for the Brother Superior in the vestibule with the polished mahogany chairs and shining brass knobs. The superior eventually bundled through the door in a bit of a flush. He had been busy in the school dealing with an 'incident'.

'You haven't heard?' he said dispensing with any niceties.

'Heard what?'

The superior shared conspiratorial looks with the old brother who had opened the door and who had reappeared.

'Brother Marías had gone a bit... well odd.'

'How do you mean *odd*?'

'He locked himself in his room for a number of weeks. He rarely came out and spoke to no one.'

'Is he still there?' Paul said. 'Can I see will he speak to me?

The superior didn't answer but looked to the statue of Saint Anthony in the alcove as if asking for guidance.

In the intervening years Brother Marías, it seemed, had became more and more reclusive, misanthropic, some said and he shunned human society— a double whammy locked inside in his little room in the already shackled monastery. They found him after breakfast one bright morning when the Brother Superior said he would have to end this 'adolescent sulking' and they forced open the door of his room. They found him hanging from a plant hook which he had fixed to the ceiling suspended by the cumberband of his soutane.

When Paul learned of Brother Marías' hanging in his dorm, all the previous suppressed emotions rose up from depths inside him like an erupting volcano. He cried out, 'No no,' and he proceeded to twist his hair into knots, a resurging habit he had as a child whenever he was angry or frustrated. Two of the Brothers tried to calm him, 'Quiet. Brother.' but there was no touch, no comforting embrace. Paul more than ever in his life at that moment longed for— had a right to demand— someone to touch him rather than cold marble beads or chalk statues or sterile missal pages; and yet that black leather-bound missal with the cross zip which his mother had bought him tied him still in its ritual.

And a page that was torn out of a tome Paul found strewn on the floor of Brother Marías' room. It was something Paul was not familiar with, something Brother Marías had never shown him: a detail from Botticelli depicting the seventh circle of hell from Dante's Inferno, portraying naked men going around in circles in anguish.

'Pray for him, Brother,' the Brother Superior said. 'We are all weak.' And that was the moment Paul knew, for he wanted to be weak and not carry on the pretence of trying to be strong anymore. He turned and looked for the last time into the bloated self-righteous face of the Brother Superior before walking away.

Why did he lose his faith? That is if faith is something to be lost, or what he is increasingly coming around to thinking of it now as a construct. It wasn't just Brother Marías' dangling from the hook that caused it, no it was this total trusting. It was all a manmade conjob. People in black garbs codding gullible people up to their eyeballs, the sale pitch delivered by histrionic missionary preachers. *Missionary,* even the terror-filled term is questionable. But that winter's day when Brother Marías came in open-toed sandals to his classroom looking for vocations, that was something to marvel at. He was gentle, he was not pushy like others, he just drew you in like Jesus with his hand beckoning, he wasn't trying to win brownie points. Paul wanted to go the same *camino* as Brother Marías. Brother Marías followed Thomas à Kempis in his *Imitation of Christ* and Paul followed Brother Marías like a magnet drawn to his kindness and gentleness. Brother Marías was a socialist, a liberation theologian before his time, before the term was even coined. He felt deeply for the poor and the havenots, particularly of those in his own country after the civil war and in South America which he was always on about. But his own life was incomplete and Paul, on different occasions, found him silently weeping in a corridor in the chapel or wherever he thought he was alone, and Paul's heart surged, but he did not know what to do to help a grown man who shed tears. After Brother Marías died, Paul was left with an aching absence in his heart; something had been ripped out of him. He thought of his paintings. He turned to Brother Marías' book.

Brother Marías had loved a boy and he was told it was not healthy to develop such close bonds with any one person. He must love all equally, the whole world. That fateful night he was reprimanded and told not to communicate with the boy again.

Inside the pages of *The Imitation of Christ*, a rose petal was pressed.

Brother Marías' passing was recorded in the obituary columns as death by natural causes. He was not buried in the Brothers' plot near the monastery, and despite repeated enquiries to the order, Paul could not discover where the remains of Brother Marías lay. They would not tell him. Why should they tell such a one. They don't reveal such information to the public. But I was his friend, Paul said. You are an apostate, the voice said and the phone went dead.

On a dark evening he visited the Brothers' plot in the cemetery in the hope of locating Brother Marías' resting place in case they had been lying to him and he thought of the *noche oscula* of Brother Marías and he remembered Brother Marías had handsome editions of the poetry of San Juan de la Cruz and the life of Santa Teresa de Ávila, a friend and mystic like him and with whom she communicated. There was a picture of the saint on the front cover, her veil and eyes directed upwards as if that was where her god lay. San Juan de la Cruz interested Paul because he was a poet, because he talked about love, about the *amada con el amado transformado* the transformation of lover into beloved, the saint wandering until he found his beloved Jesus, just as Paul wandered now, a reverend brother wading through the depths of darkness with no star or moon, just an enclosing blackness like a total despair, what Brother Marías must have felt. If he travelled with Jesus through the dark night the beloved could be transformed into the godhead as one ecstatic entity of love. Oh that was his dearest wish, or at least it was the wish of Brother Marías except...except the longed-for union was not with god but with the boy.

And he Paul is not a soul. There is no soul and he does not have the comfort that San Juan had of finding his beloved, no more than Brother Marías had because of the love of a boy.

In between headstones with no sign of the Brother's name he is suddenly waylaid and caught by a sharp blow to the head— a creature of the night knocking him to the ground. 'Who is it?' he calls out but the shadow whooshes past the headstone. Someone who does not want him there. Or just some malcontent? He gets up, dazed but not concussed, only a little suffering he concludes compared to the great torments of others.

18

'These tools will not make you,' he says situating the easel and gaining in confidence now. 'No, I'll make you from organs and sinews and ... synapses and tissues and liver and blood and marrow and eyes directing and hands acting and all—'

'All?'

'All that is inside me I will use it to make you.'

She is about to say something when he has to excuse himself. 'Gotta answer the call.'

'Are you dying, Paul?'

'Dying to go ha ha.'

'You're not going to die on me Pablo, are you, not yet? I won't allow it.'

The presumption of the surgeon Mr somebody with the tight haircut, a mortal god of that he did not... that he at his age, what age is that? And he checked his chart: it was rote learning the same spat for a hundred others, but time is of the essence with consultants. They measure out their time in scalpels. And at Paul's age he was saying in not so many words, Paul knew, that there would be no more desire.

'But you would be alive,' he said when Paul expressed his reservations.

Paul felt small and crinkled and insignificant as he walked out of the surgeon's consultancy room, unable to submit himself to this man's godlike control of his body through human interference. No matter how old it may be, his body was not a commodity; it was his with all its component parts.

'Better to be open,' he says to Viviana on returning from the bathroom.

'Open?'

'To the last chance saloon.'

Cancer progress form, PSA, Gleason score and stage: low intermediate, high slow growing, sitting quietly, urologist, oncologist. The reason he did not open the letter which still lies sealed on the kitchen table in his Dublin flat, was because he knew what it contained, bad news: digital rectal examination, they had previously told him the side effects: incontinence returning him to the baby stage, and erectile dysfunction, to get that, imagine of a prostatectomy even before it got a head start to function at all. No way, let them wait before they do that to him.

'The shape of a walnut, he said not the shape of a pea.'

'Pablo.'

'Let's skip it now okay.'

'You remind me so much of my father,' she says, 'with your refusal to—'

'Your father yes, you said that before.'

'You are offended.'

'No.'

'You *are* offended. I can see it in you, but I want to tell you he had that problem too. In fact it was that which finally— '

'I don't want to hear it,' Paul says about to walk away.

'No, please hear me out. That's why we never moved from that peasant village, because he died, Paul, at the age of forty-four from prostate cancer.'

Paul shifts. He does not want to listen to any more of this. And yet...

'So we were left, my mother and I, almost destitute stuck in a hole. And all he left to me were his dreams.'

***

He is seated on the white autobús urbano heading for the old Moorish village of A— the movement from the bus helping to dispel depressing thoughts of Viviana's father which he knew would resurrect preoccupation with his own prostate troubles. The driver exhibits great dexterity in manoeuvring the vehicle up the winding mountainous slope. When Paul disembarks at the hillside terminus there are some elderly tourists checking the return times with the bus driver, and Paul makes his way down the hill and through the narrow streets of the village. He calls to a taberna and enquires for the family name of Gutiérrez, and a wizened man appears from behind a newspaper to tell him there is an old woman, very decrepit— and he raises his hand as if to mark the furrows on his face— living alone *en la casa de la Vieja*, a house that dates back to the time before the big migration to south America in the lean days of the thirties when the poverty was so bad houses were just abandoned with many chattels still remaining with uncleared tables and uncleaned hearths as if the owners had just gone away for the day. But she is still living there, la Vieja. And some of the other houses are being filled now by families dispossessed by the fires—one of Javier's makeshift arrangements, Paul thinks, no doubt as minister.

These abandoned houses attracted hippies in the sixties, the wizened man told Paul—perhaps the types Señora Mendoza despised— giving the whole village a sort of decadent look with long greying-haired ageing guys sitting in chairs outside their little houses watching the world go by.

It is at quite an altitude up a deep and winding narrow road, the wall at the side painted white as indeed most of the houses are also with no frontage to protect them from the roadway.

There is a lattice wrought iron grid on the windows of the house and a little blue marble plaque on the outside declaiming its name. As he approaches the door of the cottage which looks out on the street he notices a bell like a shop's bell except smaller made of pewter. The string with its hanging lead he duly pulls to render a surprisingly loud church-like peal.

Despite the loudness of the peal there is no immediate response. He considers ringing again but thinks it would be impolite and he waits and eventually, after several minutes, a silver-haired ancient woman under a heavy black shawl, appears. She is tiny and bony with the skeleton of herself almost jutting out of her body and he has to look down upon her. Did people like that live? he conjectured. He was old, but he was a young fellow compared to her.

'What do you want, *forastero*?' she says in a a hoarse, craggy voice shrill as a crow's. 'You trouble an old lady to get her out of her bed for what?'

The woman's hands, which she flays about as if making up for the weakness in her voice, are marked and blotched like a leprosy. She speaks slowly in faltering *castellano*. Sometimes the ends of her words are so feebly uttered that they just seem to etherise into the atmosphere.

'I am sorry for troubling you.'

'I should be in a safer place than this.'

'I don't mean you any harm.'

'There are vandals and robbers I have to contend with. My bread was stolen outside my door. Can you believe it? The *panadero* no longer leaves it there. And those long-haired *forasteros*, are you one of those? Except...' she looks at Paul as if for the first time through rheumy eyes, 'you don't have long hair.'

'No.'

'But you are not young.'

'No, I—'

'But younger than me oh yes, I am older than a century, you know that? Why does god keep me alive I do not know. He should have taken me long ago. Maybe it was because I was waiting for my son. He went away.'

'Brother Marías.'

'You knew him?'

Paul shows her a drawing he had done of Brother Marías on a sunny day in the monastery garden when Brother Marías was planting some shrubs.

'Come in,' she says and Paul follows her into a darkened kitchen where she fetches her glasses from a table

'*Dios mío*. You did this drawing?'

'Yes.'

'They are his eyes. Always so sad.'

'I was in the monastery with him,' Paul says.

'*En Irlanda*.'

'*Sí, en Irlanda*.'

'I remember, yes he spoke of *Irlanda*, but I can't remember if it was good or bad.'

'He gave me your address before...'

'Ah yes, the monastery where he went. In one of his last letters to me, he spoke of a young person whom he loved. He took a risk to tell me, to write it down. There are always spies or else busybodies. There are always those lurking about. But there was some problem I think he had with the authorities in that country *en Irlanda* yes, the religious authorities. There are always authorities, aren't there?'

She ponders looking upwards towards the time-darkened pine joists of the ceiling. 'Yes, that is what it was, he was not allowed to love. I think that made him more sad than what he already had been. Ah mi,' she says sitting down in an old thread-worn armchair in a corner, 'is it not strange, señor that in a congregation where he did so many good things, so many good deeds, but none allowed in the name of love? Can you tell me, señor, what kind of congregation was that.'

Paul hesitates, not quite knowing what to say. All he can come out with is, 'Your son was a good man, señora. He was my mentor. He spoke of this place, his home place.'

'Mi hijo.'

'Yes.'

'Siempre perturbado.'

'Yes.'

She offers to return the drawing.

'You keep it,' Paul says.

'Thank you, señor. That is kind of you. Doing such a thing for an old unfulfilled *madre'*.

'Let me place it somewhere so you can look at it.'

'That would be nice,' she says, 'somewhere near the light.'

Paul props the drawing behind two bowls of olives on the marble kitchen top.

'Would you like some olives?' she says. 'Please take some.'

'Thank you,' he says choosing a couple of dark-coloured ones.

'I eat them every day,' she says taking one from the open bowl. 'They keep me alive, except for the stone,' she adds removing it with a look of disdain and placing it in the bowl. 'That stone will catch in my throat some day and finish me off. Maybe not a bad thing, what?'

Paul smiles. 'I hope not.'

'*Mi bambino*,' she exclaims, fixing on the drawing and proceeding to cradle in her arms an imaginary baby. 'It is many years since I have heard from him. *Ah mi. Marías* you say. That was not his name but María. His second name, not uncommon. Juan María but no one ever called him Juan. He had to leave

Spain because of Franco, because of what Franco did to *mi marido*, his *padre*, you understand. Terrible things, terrible things happened then, thrown into the filthy overcrowded prison of Tarragona with a thousand others who opposed Franco. He was arrested delivering a coded message to his superiors saying a delivery of seed potatoes were about to arrive, in other words hand grenades. But that prison they threw him into was built to hold only a hundred. Ay mi, can you imagine what that must have been like. *Mi marido* almost suffocated. He could not breathe the foul air. My son, even at a young age, was valiant and loved his *padre*. He tried to spring his escape with some friends, sympathisers, republican you know. They tried to arrange his escape from that accursed prison. One of the comrades killed a prison guard in the process and they opened the prison door and hundreds of prisoners filed out and fled including *mi marido*, hiding in the countryside. But the guardías civiles pursued them and with the aid of an informer located and shot most of them, *fusilado* you know.'

'Did your husband escape?'

'No, ay mi, but my son escaped. He fled Spain with Franco's secret agent Alonso the Butcher hot on his heels.'

'Alonso, you say.'

'Oh yes, the Butcher of Tarragona, and his son the big shot minister now, the *vecino* who should have been our ally betraying his own. Gave their names to the guardías civiles. Anyone who spoke against the caudillo was listed. I will never forget his name. Got high up in the government, Franco's right hand man climbing the mountain of dead bodies to get to the top. *Mi pobre hijo* hid in barns and woods and made his way north to the coast to Santander when an order of Irish, your country yes, Irish Christian Brothers gave him refuge. They did not ask which side he was on. They just saw a man in need.'

She stops to regard Paul. 'And you were his friend, yes?'

'Yes,' Paul says. 'Did he write to you?'

'Write to me, you say. How could he write or speak or tell the true story. It would give him away. He got word of himself back to me through a network of sympathetic travellers, but, ay mi, they have all gone or passed away now, But look at me, señor, just left here. Why? Why am I left here? I go out in the morning before the sun gains in strength and get my few things, simple things, olives and bread which can no longer be delivered because of thieves, and then come back to my sepulchre. Yes this is how I exist like a living dead when everyone else is gone. All shadows now. And sometimes,' she says and he can sense her reaching down deep into the well of her memory, 'he would send me postcards signing off as my nephew. And one of the authorities when censoring my post even commended me on having "a nephew" in the religious life.'

'But when Franco died... was there not...?'

'You think Franco has gone? I am not so sure. There will always be his spies about like the Butcher. Do you know we were not even allowed into the graveyard of our beloved deceased, blocked out by barbed wire. We used to weep at the boundary wall.'

'And this Butcher...?'

'In a hospital, a nursing home for the old and decrepit where I will wind up soon enough. But please god not in the same place as him. And his big shot son goes to visit him there, I have been told. That man who has the blood of many on his hands including María's father, my beloved husband.'

And Paul wonders is it possible that it is the butcher and not his son that Viviana wants him to help her to rid the world of. But if that is the case how could she possibly believe that he could do such a thing? Does she see the crimes lurking inside her spouse carrying the poisonous genes?

'Even then he feared that he or I could be put on trial, could be judged retrospectively, as so many were. The civil war you know did not end the killings. He was a most vindictive man, Franco. He pursued his enemies and murdered them long after the war was over. Do you know what it was like señor, have you any idea what it was like to live on tenterhooks, to look over your shoulder and wonder who is for you and who is against you, who is ready to put a knife in your back?'

And Paul thinks, yes he did have some idea as San Salvador looms before him; all wars are the same in their inhumanity.

'It had happened with other families,' she continues, her voice faint forcing Paul to stoop towards her to hear. 'Betrayal is so vile you cannot trust anyone and your neighbours least of all. It was his fear all his life, but was it a life hiding away from himself and from me? *Ay mi*. As a boy he was estrange, a figure apart, a friend to birds and the animals like Saint Francis of Assisi. You have heard of him?'

'Yes.'

'He had a book about Saint Francis. He wanted to be like him. He always collected religious books and mass brochures. He would wander through the pews after mass picking up the pamphlets and he loved gold plaited pages and colourful scripts and the trees, he loved the trees. He wanted to join his order, but instead he had a summons from god calling him to South America, to go there, that he was needed there to help the downtrodden people. But was that really a call or some make believe thing? I sometimes wonder, señor. He did not write letters to me.'

And Paul thinks how fortunate he was that he deigned to write them to him.

'Perhaps he felt they would incriminate him or me with the authorities.' She grabs her throat. 'My voice is going, señor. Can you fetch me a glass of water from the *jarra* on the table.'

'Don't you think that he is right?' she says sipping unsteadily from the glass which Paul hands to her. When you think of it, any semblance of joy we ever had, came from the pain of living.'

'I suppose there is some truth in that,' Paul says.

'Some truth ha. Don't talk about truth please. Whose truth? Your truth, my truth, the Francoist truth. What is truth, my friend but a man's distortion of reality.'

'Sorry I...'

'But my son did not see that. He was an absolutist you understand, and that was the sacrifice he made, the pain leading to the ecstasy that he sought so much to be in union with Santa Teresa and San Juan.'

She hands the glass back to Paul.

'Open that drawer,' she says pointing toward a desk by the window under the marble vanity top. Paul goes to the drawer and takes out a bundle of colour postcards with stamps marked Guatemala, Venezuela, Chile, Bolivia, Paraguay and El Salvador.

Just post cards with religious images of the Virgin or Cristo on the Cross or pictures of some saint got from cathedrals or churches. A lot of the pictures, Paul notes, depict human suffering or some ecstasy as a result of it, except for a Hinde postcard caught in the mix from Ireland showing rhododendrons in bloom.

'I don't know why he stopped sending me the postcards. Perhaps he became *perturbado*— the sadness of the world you know, he felt it so strongly, *mi pobrecito*.'

'He stopped writing to me as well,' Paul says.

'To you, he wrote to you?'

'Yes. When I was in San Salvador.'

'You were there too?'

'Yes, with the Brotherhood.'

'His *madre* he was forgetting about. Perhaps he had his sights fixed on another world.'

'Yes, that would be him. He helped the poor in South America. He did very important work there. The world owes a gratitude to your son.'

She sighs. 'But what good is it helping the world and neglecting his mother?'

'Not wilfully,' Paul says. 'He became ill and was sent back to the mother house in Ireland.'

'His mother's house was here,' she says thumping her heart. 'And you were his friend.'

'Yes.'

'His friend that he loved.'

'Yes.'

Paul feels tears welling.

Her lips quiver as if she is trying to articulate something. 'And then the telegram came. Oh I will never forget that day, you know like those telegrams that used to come during the war informing *madres* and *novias* in the briefest possible way with sincere sympathy. How can we tell it was sincere with dry words on a page? The reverend or was it the revered —my memory lets me down. Reverend Brother Superior, yes that word Superior, that's what it was. We regret to inform you that your son passed away. And the date was given, that was all.'

'A telegram is limited in words,' Paul says trying to assuage her hurt.

'Ay mi. A son dying before his mother. It is not right. Something is amiss. I was too old to travel of course. I asked that the body be sent home.'

'And it was?'

'Yes. Only a little while ago, a little piece of time in our mortal world. It arrived, the coffin containing the remains of my son arrived like cargo at Reus airport?' She stops to catch her breath and, wheezing, says, 'It was good at least that he was buried in his *patria*, don't you think?'

'Yes,' Paul says and he thinks how convenient it was for the congregation to get rid of the body in such a manner—just export it and banish the problem.

'When days are serene you know señor, I am peaceful, but there was a chill in my bones with the aeroplane descending. No reverend brother to accompany it, just some official in a dark suit who seemed to be in a great hurry to be shut of the body, my son, to be shut of him. All he wanted was the signing of paper and he was off. There was no great pity there. So we buried María, all the good neighbours who remembered him. They came together to welcome my son home. And the old men remembered his exploits, hailing him as a hero, and they buried him beside his father. And there was another new grave there freshly dug beside his. You know of the tragic case of the young fisherman?'

'Yes,' Paul says and he remembers seeing no graveyard in the small fishing village. The funeral yes took place there but the cemetery was here.

'Ah yes, how estrange,' the Vieja continues, 'the young man not drowned in the sea as it is the way with many fisherman but burned in the great fire. You saw the fires?'

'Yes.'

'The *pobrecito*, his life stretching before him.'

'It was tragic,' Paul says.

'Ah my son,' she says breathing heavily, 'he was confused in his head. He used to ask me questions like how come religion is good, Mamá and Franco who goes to Mass is bad? That was a conflict he carried with him. And his father whom he loved, but was a republican, he hardly knew, taken before he could understand the world. But in his brief life his father was always kind to him and he felt duty-bound, you understand. But his father's death weighed heavily on him. And many wondered how it was that he had died and I am still alive, still existing, reversing the order of things don't you think, a mother outliving her son?'

'Did he, I mean the official, give a cause of death for your son?'

'No, I cannot recall any record. It is strange. I cannot tell you how my son died, only that he died suddenly. No señor, I cannot tell how he died but I can tell you why he died.'

'You know?'

'It was because he did not have the heart to live anymore. The *corazón* you know,' she says touching her breast, 'is such a delicate organ. Not like me, not like his *madre* whose heart is made of old tautened leather.'

19

The pain, more a discomfort in the penial gland, had eased in recent weeks as he continued eating pumpkin seeds with assorted nuts in his morning cereal, grounded down with a blender he had purchased in the local *supermercado*, for his remaining teeth would not be able for that kind of grinding any more.

But now the urine flow is slow, drip drip. The pain is back. What is he doing with this nubile woman? She thinks he is handsome. She sees the residue of handsomeness in his face. That's all it is, a residue and yet enough to attract her, vain creature. But not enough, he knows. Face up to it, you are an old man and she has some ulterior motive. Oh, but the desire in him is still so strong.

He waits impatiently for the gate to open. How much of our life is waiting, wondering what if, what now, what was. He looks at his watch as if he can recapture past time. A touch of despair striking in the dimly lit corridor, that penumbra seizing one. The sound of a bell in a distant past. Where has she gone? It is the appointed time of 11 am. Punctuality is something he is good at, has been well trained in, and he cannot quite understand the lack of it in others. How unpleasant to be locked out. He has left his sketches in her room. But now the gate opens and he sees her, and tears well not so much for the seeing of her but for the memory. How much worse it always was, to be locked in.

Ignominy, she used that word in passing. He can't even remember the context exactly. There was no context come to think of it, she just murmured it, exhaled it through her half-closed lips, her breath encapsulating the word, the concept in the atmosphere. And then she flails as if possessed and says, 'Tomorrow.'

And he says, 'Tomorrow? But I have just arrived. It is the appointed time.'

'No no,' she says. 'Today I have a film shoot.'

But as Paul looks around, there is no one about other than Conchita who (under curt orders), proceeds, albeit reluctantly, to escort him out.

'Is there really a film shoot?' he asks Conchita, who simply sighs and turns her eyes up to heaven.

And he endures Viviana's voice shouting after him. 'When I was younger I was trying to find God in all things, like you. I read Gerard Manly Hopkins and thought of dappled things. Now I am just trying to find things. Ah, what is the world? Can you hear me?'

***

A daily or regular diary entry helps him to keep abreast of himself when his mind is wandering off, to catch it, to draw it in. The mind does wander, likes to follow its own paths and seeks, like the body, its own gratification. He is preaching now even if only to himself — order the word, but order yes out of chaos, find it, the role of the artist. Saint Ignatius tells us that God deals directly with the 'well-disposed person'. But how does he know who is well-disposed, and disposed for what? Such presumption. How does anyone know? All we know is the natural course of things The laws of attraction. Every cell in the human body vibrates. What of the skin? Made of powerful magnets. One's vibes attract or repulse. Better in the end to surrender oneself to limitlessness.

The senses. She spoke about the senses or just one sense really when she went on about the sense of touch. But what of the others? Mentioning Hopkins as he was going out the door, shouting it after him, did she know he had been a priest? And talking of dappled things, how well read she was.

The senses, yes.

What does he see? The mountain, the sea, the naked lady.

What does he hear? The waves rolling, human laughter.

What does he taste? Bitterness, the taste of an orange, the old acidity.

What does he smell? Wood smoke in a distant childhood place, charcoal the link, her perfume wafting through the night air.

What does he feel? Ah, the most important sense to which all the others are subservient. What does he feel? A medley, was that the word she used?

The next morning she is sitting at the patio table and shuffling cards. 'I like dealing,' she says, not bothering to greet him and behaving as if he had never gone away, 'but not playing'. She throws them out on the glass table seeing will the ace of spades come up. And it does invariably after a shuffle or two. She seems almost happy with this bizarre and, in his mind, childish game. He refrains from mentioning anything about her supposed film shoot for fear she would in one of her mood swings have second thoughts about going through with the posing, and that word *ignominy,* could it be possible that she was developing a latter-day bashfulness?

'That means death,' she says proffering the card, and when he looks at her gloating, the desire for her in him lessens and the contortion in her face reminds him of a demoniacal witch. How can it be, someone so beautiful? What is it that lies hidden perhaps in all of us if only the key were to be found?

The blue pigment has hardened in its jar. The night was relatively cold and he remembers, Brother Marías telling him one time what to do in such an incident: he places the jar in a bowl of warm water and walks away patient to wait for its liquefying.

'Could I tell this story with pictures alone.'

'A story? You mean a pictorial narrative about my life?'

'Perhaps.'

'A theatre of images.'

'The painting could be in the form of globes. There could be a back and a front and a face and a derriere.'

'Oh of course the derriere.'

'A framed painting has its limitations.'

'You can't see around the corner.'

'Exactly. For then it would be no different to the framed photograph, both enclosed, both rectangular, enclosures like ranches corralling the beasts.'

'Wow.'

'Too strong, the memory of the cloister. Don't fence me in, the song.'

'Perhaps you would consider an untypical exhibition. With all the mod cons.'

'There may be an art gallery in Dublin who would be mildly interested.'

'In buttocks?'

'Not just buttocks. More curvatures. The enticing anatomy of curves. Besides I also have landscapes and—'

'To distract.'

'And oils on linen.'

'Linen?'

'Yes, I'm trying it out, sketching as you know first in charcoal.'

'Yes, those grey Irish colours like your skies.'

'And watercolours.'

'Of course. Why not?'

'And then over several weeks hopefully completing in oil.'

'Mona Lisa was no oil painting.'

'Ha, ha.'

'Collage.'

'Yes.'

'Photographs.'

'Perhaps.'

'Paper clippings.'

'What?'

'Something instinctual.'

'To operate fully under instinct is a luxury only the animals can enjoy. Where did I read that?'

'Are we not animals?'

'Don't tell me too many things,' he says surprising himself by his increasing frankness. He is in the middle of trying to capture her left high cheek bone. It is not coming along too well. It's exaggerated, his rendition. It shouldn't be that high. It's like he is trying to confer on her an aristocracy that maybe isn't there. She had been rattling on, people and their locutions, about the paparazzi, and the words were jumbled in his head like that part of his eighty billion brain cells were not turned on the listening part, this was the part of seeing.

'You are supposed to be my muse.'

'Not muse, model.'

She was not meant to act like a garrulous spouse harping on the mundanities no matter how real, no matter how significant they were, intruding on his fixation.

'You want me to be quiet,' she says noticing his frown.

'If you wouldn't mind. Just till I finish this part. Your cheek bone is proving—'

'Cheeky.'

How well she knows the English nuances and his mind now brings back the words, and that other part of his brain is cranked into awareness strangulating that elusive part that can only come so rarely and with surprise; that he was accustomed to lie like a poet (for that is what he is beginning to feel he is: a brush poet) in solitary waiting whenever inspiration will deem to arrive, knowing that no amount of cajoling or pleading can induce it.

'Are you finished already?' she says, seeing him folding up his easel.

The next morning he sits by the open French door staring out at the pool conscious of sweat trickling down the side of his now tanned face. Something is stopping him from wiping it away. Why bother? He had to rouse himself from his bed with the previous day's unsuccessful efforts still lurking in his brain.

'You look tired, Pablo. Are you okay?'

'Most of what we do is mimetic,' he says coldly. 'That is the problem, isn't it, all images are old images.'

Looking over his shoulder at the aborted cheek frame which he is about to discard, she says, 'This working in sections... perhaps you could...'

'Perhaps I could what?'

'Forgive me I am not the artist here.'

'Say what you want.'

'I mean could you perhaps work in broader sweeps? I mean cheek bones is not the person, is it?'

'Cheek bones, derriere, noses, eyes, ears, which are the most beautiful? Pick one, have a choice, legs, breasts.'

'I didn't mean to anger you.'

He rises and shrugs. 'The body is fragmented for effect. It will all come together in the end I hope. In the meantime I have to isolate. Don't you understand, digging to get to the atom, you know what you talked about. So forgive me if I appear irritating.'

'I didn't t say anything about atoms,' she says.

'Oh for god sake. I mean to find all the components and then put them all together.'

'In the right order of course.'

She is mocking, he knows.

'I mean,' she says clicking her vape, 'who determines the order, Pablo?'

'I don't understand you.'

'Sometimes I think...'

'What?'

'Sometimes I think the body is a limitation.'

He remains silent, holding his easel, examining her with his eyes, wondering who she really is.

He does call to her two days later, but it is another day and no work. A sulk, he suspects, may have descended on her as if she is seeking vengeance for his sharpness towards her. But no reason is given by Conchita who merely directs her eyes towards heaven once more and tells him to call another day when the señora will be feeling better.

When he does call the following morning she continues her sulk.

'I cannot capture you if you keep staring like that.'

She doesn't answer but pouts her lips like an adolescent no better than Maribel. And he wonders if her behaviour has nothing to do with him at all. Maybe it has more to do with Javier or Maribel or her own frustrated dreams or even due to her medication gone awry.

And then, 'You're the artist, make the art.'

It's a challenge, she is throwing down a gauntlet.

'How can I try?' he says staring at the blank canvas which he has just mounted on the easel. 'What I seek is the erotic inherent in the form, to make the paint work as flesh, but it is so easy to say such a thing, is it not, but so hard to execute. The guilt is what is blocking me.'

'I thought it was my chatter.'

'That perhaps too but to a lesser extent.'

'Thank you.'

'But the guilt, all the years, they are the shackles holding back the art.'

'And holding up your trousers too,' she says mockingly

'All I have,' he says dismissing the barb, 'is a lifetime of accumulated ignorance to draw from.'

'Are you procrastinating, Pablo? I mean we can leave it.'

'Leave it?'

'If it's too much for you. This undertaking, this grand scheme of yours.'

'It's not a grand scheme. On the contrary it's trying to break down grand schemes.'

'Maybe you should go back and stick to the smaller works, the illustrations you did for the books, the lives of the saints. Maybe I am too much for you.'

He looks up, it's overcast the sky. Helios has not come out today.

20

'What I had to deal with,' Javier says cowering down without any of the niceties of introduction as Paul arrives at the restaurant table where Javier is already seated.

Javier had phoned Paul—his secretary had got the number of the apartment— said he had to speak to him and would send his chauffeur to pick him up. They agreed to meet discreetly at a quiet afternoon time in the restaurant in the hills overlooking the town.

The chauffer, a small squat man with a thick neck was inquisitive, wanting to know all about Paul. Paul retorted with quick evasive answers and was glad when the journey ended.

Javier looks distraught when Paul sees him. His hair, for what remains of it, is straggly and his eyes are watery.

'You said you have stuff to deal with,' Paul says

'Sit down please,' he says and Paul, giving a cursory smile to the waitress, pulls up a chair.

'You are a kindly man, a heroic man and I feel I can confide in you.'

'You flatter me.'

'No, please hear me out. When you saved my daughter's life, it made me feel like you are part of my *familia* now. I can surely trust you with the circumstances of my own unhappy life.'

'Thank you,' Paul says uncomfortable with such praises, 'but I—.'

'You have some idea now,' he says sternly holding Paul in a stare, 'what my wife is like.'

'Perhaps I am learning.'

There is a shake in Javier's coffee cup as he holds it to his lips. 'My wife is changeable like the seasons. I am sure you agree she is beautiful. Of course you do, otherwise why would you be painting her? I was her scapegoat, her stool pigeon.'

He lowers his head into his hands. 'She hisses at me like a feral cat. She wants to bring me down, bring us all down. And she has created this myth about herself.'

'A myth?'

'I am part of the myth. I am the bad guy, and many people believe it because of my father. But I cannot atone for the sins of my father. They were times in history, my friend. People did strange things then. They were forced and cajoled to the strains of war.'

He raises his head to regard Paul more stoically now. 'But at least Maribel doesn't think I am a bad guy. And thank god for that. Have you spoken to that poor girl? How she has suffered. It was her mother's cigarette lighter you know which caused all the damage. She is the reason now why Maribel is blind...'

'Ah surely not,' Paul interrupts.

'The doctors have confirmed her condition is irreversible.'

'I am so sorry to hear that,' Paul says.

'The villagers know about the lighter and the boy's uncle knows. Conchita—'

'Conchita, she told them?' Paul says.

'You are astute, my friend. Perhaps you are right. I do not know for certain. Conchita would neither confirm nor deny. My wife, you may have noticed, does not treat Conchita very well.'

'I have noticed,' Paul says.

Viviana wanted to dismiss her, but Conchita was always very good with Maribel, especially when she was small, and I insisted she stay. But anyway, getting back to the matter of the lighter, Viviana feels the worry now and I could be implicated, well not so much me but her. She torments me all the time to use my influence to get the damned lighter back. The police have it, investigating you know. But I could not do that my friend, despite her ranting and raving at me. I could not interrupt the police in their enquiries. It would not be right. It would not be seen to be right.'

'So that may account for the mood swings.'

'You have noticed.'

'Yes.'

'Oh, she always had them. But if she had been more amenable to Maribel and her beau, things could have been different, less tragic. They could've entertained one another in the villa instead of having to hide away from her disapproving gaze. She didn't want Maribel dating the young man, saying he wasn't good enough for her, a mere *paisono*. That was the word she used. She didn't want anyone or anything threatening her own ego. I never knew till after I had married her that she couldn't stand anyone else stealing her limelight, even her own daughter having a chance of happiness, a chance of love.'

He sighs as if that last phrase was an afterthought. 'But she has put it out there that I am the bad guy whereas the truth—'

'The truth?'

'Yes the truth. It was I who encouraged her when she failed all those auditions. Did she tell you about her failures with those producer fellows? And god knows how she abased herself to try to win their favour, and one particular fellow who took full advantage and left her high and dry with a bucket load of empty promises that he would make her a star. But the truth is they found her too cerebral. They did not want a woman like her despite her looks. I tried to pull her away from all that superficial world and I was amazed, how a woman of her intelligence succumbed to its wiles. But that was her weakness all along: vanity. Yes, she was the most vain creature, even as a child, always seeking praise. But she never thanked me.'

Paul sees no villainy in this man no matter how hard he tries. Javier is not a villain. What goes on behind closed doors between a husband and a wife he cannot tell. How could he tell? But more and more he is becoming inclined towards the husband as the maligned one, and he agrees a son cannot be blamed for the sins of a father ('She says I got into politics under my father's coat tails but it is not true, my friend. I worked hard for my position').

And this promiscuity which Viviana exhibits (even if gratifyingly towards him and for which he is indeed grateful), but a wife who shows no loyalty to a faithful husband is contrary to all he was led to believe about a true marriage, and he finds himself despising Viviana in equal measure to his adoration of her.

And, as for Javier, he feels uncomfortable in his presence. Should he say something to him, admit about the increasing intimacies with his wife? He feels he is betraying this honest man.

'Javier,' he says.

'What is it, my friend?'

21

Who wandered in high mountains? What dispossessed families without refuge? Children wailing. What is it like to be without a home. The homeless of Dublin's streets and the streets of Sao Paulo he witnessed first-hand, and now here in the land of Helios, families passing, funerals, how many today have passed by on the street cut off from traffic? And hundreds of people walking behind hearses, heads down in lamentation in the universal cry of human suffering since time immemorial, the lot, the human condition, the dead will always be with us. Better a quick death than what some have suffered, a slow roasting. Like the cooked flesh for a restaurant, a rich repast, eat my body—the Crucifixion and then the cannibalism— the raw (to borrow from Viviana's lexicon) and the cooked, the weeping of the living for the annihilation of the damned, Guernica fate, and a human hand that started the fire.

Maribel is standing biting her lip by the flower bed, her arms wrapped around a posy of blue and white flowers. She is dressed in a loose white linen dress edged in blue and, seeing her, he can think of nothing other than the Virgin, the blue and white flowers for the May altar. But the reality: Maribel is blind and does not believe in anything other than the scent of the flowers which she is holding to her nose now. How a perception can clothe a person unwittingly. He is watching from behind his easel, the desire to go to her, to talk to her, to try her one more time. But why trouble her in her moment of rapture, so rare those moments must be for her? A sense not lost. She raises her head towards the rising sun and sighs as if the rapture has ended and, turning around, retreats indoors.

Overcome with feeling of such sympathy for Maribel, he abandons his easel and, seeing no sign of Viviana or Conchita, he leaves the villa and makes his way to the fishing village thinking of the fish caught in the net, the Bible played out for real. People gather to buy the fish direct from the *pescadores* before their price increase through the retail. Women carry loaves and fresh rolls from the *panadería,* and now the first lobster and crab and cod to accompany the bread, the earth and the sea in its abundance feeding all.

The curled grey-haired *pescador*, the uncle of the boy Angelo, has berthed his modest blue fishing boat like Saint Peter making ready to cast out once more into the deep. His sorrow whipped by the sea breeze no longer visible as he is engrossed head down with his nets or perhaps lost like so many of the other dead contained in the crashing of the waves. The nets are hoisted on decks dripping with sea water and trapped fish. The net will be cast once more, (it is the woman who is trapped) trapping all ideologies.

'Excuse me señor,' Paul says, 'but I couldn't help noticing your net hanging off the bollard on the pier is damaged.'

'It has too many holes. It is beyond repair.'

'Would it be okay if I...'

'What, you want it? Take it and be damned.'

Paul does not engage further with the uncle who seems to be in a foul mood, dwelling still no doubt on the death of his nephew. But Paul does not make himself known to him and the man does not look up for, if he had, he would surely have recognised Paul from the press photograph. So Paul thanks him for the net and leaves him, unknowing, to his own enterprise.

Further out the crags are lashed by the foam. There are few people about here. The sea is too rough, wild nature, screeching terns on rocks. And there is one larger rock protruding, overhanging the waves; it cannot be touched; it is too high up. The rock is defying the waves. The sea will fail to corrode it, to break it down. The waves are growing angrier as they cannot reach high enough to whip at that tall impervious rock. And then he sees the face as the waters recede, clearly, the face of a woman. Helios pulls back the blind of a cloud and the woman shivers in her intensity.

'Where did you go?'

'Out for some air.'

'Conchita was shopping and I was in my room, preparing for you. Why did you not knock?'

'Sorry, I...'

'Oh, forget it.'

After Paul makes several abortive efforts trying to fashion her nose, she rises to survey the canvas and exclaims, 'You are untrained, that is not a nose.'

'You are right. It is not a nose. It is the perception of a nose. Picasso's women were not women but his perception of them.'

'The qualia.'

'Exactly.

She tuts. 'I thought we had done with mister Picasso.'

'He painted Guernica.'

'Yes he painted that monstrosity.'

'It wasn't a monstrosity surely, but rather the depictions of one.'

'Whatever... He did not treat his women well, you know that.'

'Yes, I know that.'

'He just used them or abused them rather. Picasso was a bastard.'

'The conundrum,' Paul says.

'Conundrum?' she says flailing her arms, 'what conundrum?'

'Man and art. You know it was Brother Marías who trained me in my first strokes.'

'Strokes? You are a master of ambiguity, Pablo.'

Paul wipes his brush. 'You know Viviana, your English is so good, you can chide me with nuances and puns not even intended.'

'I'll take that as a compliment.'

'Brother Marías talked of pointillism. Surreptitiously of course.'

'Weren't you secretive devils in that monastery of yours?'

'He did drawings of charcoal on paper, on anything in fact he could lay his hands on.'

'Did he lay his hands on you?'

'Please, Viviana.'

'Oh sorry.'

'Open yourself, he said to me, open yourself to new forms. But despite all things, all he had were a few chalks and pencils and small paints easy to conceal. He did not advance in his artistic endeavours as he would have wished. There were always interruptions, the clanking of bells intruding on any flights of fancy we may have had.'

'So he was trapped.'

'Yes, entangled in a net. And he always reverted despite the high hopes back to the staid religion like it was a fear to wander too far away even though that was what he seemed to be suggesting, that that is what he should do.'

'Back to the religious paintings of the books.'

'Yes, when anyone else was present he extolled the icons.'

Noticing a book sticking out, she reaches for his cotton bag.

'What are you doing?'

'I want to know what the great painter is reading now? *Ars Spiritualis Inescandi Mulieres. The Spiritual Art of Enticing Women.*'

'You are familiar with this book?' he says.

'The necessary parts.'

'Of course.'

Paul was relieved she had not noticed another book at the bottom of the bag: *Crime and Punishment*. Since she mentioned the pistol, he has been reading Dostoevsky. It was a slightly dog-eared second-hand volume he had picked up in a Spanish translation in a flea market. He identifies with Raskolnikov. Like him, he feels he is undergoing an existential crisis, but his desire propels him. What is this thing that contorts his innards? This is not what it is meant to be, desire was not meant to be a murderous weapon. But you can just walk away Paul, a voice is saying. Ah sublimate, another one of those life-defying actions. Return to what remains of your sombre, boring existence and just fade into the earth without ever having known the world. Remain a nonentity, an unfulfilled person, another Brother Marías. What good did it do him, all that sublimation, all that self-denial, hiding away from the essence of his being, living a lie and then dying the way he did, the way he ended it in utter despair. Would Paul go that way too with all those unfulfilled longings, a lifetime of desires pent up and sacrificed for what? A mythical man on a cross. God makes the path of the elect with thorns. Is that all there is? If life has any meaning surely it must be an individual quest, not something preordained. How boring that would be.

There is no world beyond this one. As Nietzsche says god is dead, so what does he have to lose in surrendering himself to the pleasurable dictates of this woman, no matter what the consequences may be?

She has the wiles of Salome, how she dances behind the veil, the Moorish music coming from a small CD player playing on the glass table top. She can seduce like Delilah digging, unearthing what it is to be a man, cajole and mock and taunt until your very manhood crumbles and he is driven crazy by the siren release. There is no release until you the pristine, the old oak seeing what she can do to him, tantalising tormenting driving him mad, the reverend Brother, the old celibate, what a delight to behold the power she can exert on such a man. The trigger. But to do that Paul must become Saul. How can such a reversal take place of all our received doctrines? How can they be turned upside down? Put the Bible in motion only backwards to what the world was before humans tinkered with it. But would it not be a glorious act of truth taken in his later life after the conjob of his past? To change from an inhibited religious-bound being to that of a confident free thinking artist.

'Caravaggio killed a man, perhaps many men.'

22

They are gathered in the church of San Pedro, the patron saint of fishermen. However, their seats are not facing the altar but sideways in the transept for outsiders and separate from the locals and main congregation and making them in the eyes of Paul a display unit. Viviana does not attend, using the ironic excuse of having to mind Maribel. Javier, duly suited in charcoal hues, joins in the prayers and later stands in the queue to commiserate with the family of the boy. The uncle whispers something into the ear of the bereft mother as Javier approaches and his outstretched hand is refused.

Through the tintinnabulation of the mourners as they trudge their way out of the church, Paul is able to decipher most of the conversations despite the clipped dialect.

The mother of the boy is overwrought. She is listening to her brother, the boy's uncle declaiming. That jumped-up actress, too stuck up to attend, no respect, afraid to appear, the uncle is saying. Sí sí, say a chorus of *pescadores*. She looks down on us villagers, ordinary people of her village where she came from. Even at a young age she was a *sinvergüenza,* wrapped the local boys around her finger and Javier Alonso among them. Sí, and where he came from, bad blood, an accursed pair bringing shame to our village. Would that she had never been born.

***

The rain pounds down. Never before had he witnessed such violence of water pummelling the earth. In Ireland there is rain, always rain, but it is generally a slow steady drizzle calibrating the levels of national depression, but a cataclysm such as this as cars are washed into the sea and the streets are becoming rivers, that is a whole different ball game reflecting the passions of its people. That is a day to enter the storm into the canvas of bright light and blur the clouds that are coming in the storm, the dampener, raining on the parade in Spain.

She is huddled in a blanket and looks bemused, one dimensional in her glare.

'I'm your story, Spain.'

'I had forgotten.'

'Why this Brother Marías? she says, and he detects a note of jealousy in her voice.

'Why?'

'Yes, why?'

'He was the only man...'

'The only man? What do you mean, Pablo?'

'My father was rarely there for me. It wasn't intentional. He was a commercial traveller. He was a good man, good in so far as good has any meaning now.'

'You are changing your ethics.'

'Not changing. Losing them.' And he thinks of Raskolnikov and the novel he has finished reading. 'Isn't that what you want? Your challenge making me think of all the values that I thought I had stood for.'

'Progress then.'

'My father was a good man but not good for me.'

And so you were a little boy without a daddy. Poor Pablo. How we both suffered from our daddies. But tell me, in those dormitories what did you do, Paul? At night all alone, just you and your fictitious soul?'

'You like doing that, don't you?'

'Doing what, pray?'

'Taunting me.'

'You are such an old man, Paul. Come on, cast your mind back, a young man in puberty with an uncontrollable urge, with a stupid vow to keep you down. Tell me, Paul. Come on, tell me, the sheets rising, tell me, like a tent, a wigwam yes Paul, in your bunk bed. Was it a bunk bed? In the dark what did you do, Paul? What did your holy self allow you to do? And this Brother Marías, was he really a father figure, or was he not something different?'

'Different? What do you mean?'

She does not answer but stares knowingly at him, feeling victorious in this game of hers.

'Maybe he was different. It never got to that stage of my finding out. The love Brother Marías and I shared with one another,' he says feeling emboldened now, 'was like the love of a father and son, or perhaps what the love between a father and son should be like. It was not as hinted at by some. It was a pure love, if there is such a thing, but even that never got a chance to...'

'Develop.'

'Perhaps.'

'Like us, Pablo.'

'No, not like us, not in that sense.'

'Enough of that,' she says.

***

He remembers as a child lying in bed in his parents' suburban house staring at two pictures on his bedroom wall which his mother had hung, and he liked neither of them. The first was of a chapel on an island. It was so square and there was a lack of curves like it had not been painted at all but was mere architecture with rulers and compasses to emphasise instead of detracting from its already rectangular shape. Except perhaps for the door of the church which was open and had a totally black interior with not even the flicker of a candle emanating, suggesting that any poor misguided creature who entered was not entering into light but into a darkness. The second picture hanging a little askew was of Jesus and Mary in a predominantly pink colour. Jesus had a perm and a groomed beard and was holding his heart outside his tunic, the heart not at the side but in the middle of his chest. The Sacred Heart of Jesus, a religious icon that hypnotised and drew many to the pious life. Did it have to be so kitsch and biologically inaccurate, with an inanimate Mary standing meekly beside him? Mass-produced.

What paint did he mix to make her glow? What paint runs through her veins from the palette of her conception? Was there oozing, haemorrhaging? What veins run through the canvas? Tedious? This coming into being. What brushes did he use? What tools, hammers and pliers, did he employ to stretch her girth on canvas when drawing her eyebrows, giving his individual *sfumato?*

'You can't control me,' she says. 'You can't control the world. Don't put your pleasure above the work itself. I am covered with too many frilly bits,' she adds looking over his shoulder. 'That sea is too frothy. If you learn too much about me, it will always be about. You are going beyond me.'

'It is all in the process,' he says.

***

His mother's expectations. What does he remember?

Paul's mother was from a well-to-do devout family, the O'Dwyers of Rathgar. Her older brother Michael had been a missionary priest and he wrote frequent letters to his beloved sister about his heroic efforts —he was never shy or wavering about his God-given role to convert the heathen and the black babies of Africa. It is part of our religious duty, she told her son when he was at that impressionable young age of twelve or thirteen with ideologies and all sorts of possible worlds swilling around in his head. She would set her son down on the wine-coloured settee in their living room and read to him Michael's letters as if they were the gospel. Her voice echoed her brother's lofty sentiments. It is our duty and the duty of all good Catholics not only to attend mass and church services but it is also our sacred role to spread the word of Jesus to those poor black babies on the darkest of continents. And his mother quoted Saint Thomas from his *summa* and, despite being married herself, she taught her son what she firmly believed: that virginity was more excellent than marriage for it is precisely the infinite character of the good that the Virgin seeks— God himself, while married peoples' energies are taken up and dissipated with each other and their children.

And he never wondered about his mother and father in that context. His father was a quiet man who agreed with his wife on most things or maybe looking back on it with adult eyes it was more of a succumbing to her, for he never remembers his father arguing. Like her, he was a devout Catholic with an unquestioning faith, typical of his generation. But did he ever in his solitary moments wonder the way his wife extolled virginity or how it was Paul was ever born at all, and did his birth mark the end of his parents' intimacies? He never in all the years heard a sound from the little bedroom in the back of the house with the immersion heater in the cupboard for extra warmth except the odd time when his mother's bedside prayer could be heard mumbled or his father's transistor was on, for he loved the radio. Classical music, symphonies he liked. He did not like words in music (a trait his son inherited) as if he was seeking a symphony or sexless karma in his own life. But what of his latent desires? Did he even know he had them? Paul never knew, being away from them since such an early age. Did his father, like so many of the time, think all things of the flesh were impure, base covetousness? How can thoughts be impure of themselves? Surely it is the acting of them makes them so, and his thoughts shift to Dostoevsky again. The thinking of murder was not wrong. Can you kill for a higher good as Raskolnikov believed in killing the old contemptuous pawnbroker? Just as Paul had killed the rapist and maybe the rapist was also a plague invading a country. Raskolnikov didn't look upon the pawnbroker as a person but as an illness that was affecting good people. So what do you do with an illness, suffer on, or get better? But the pawnbroker was merely a victim of a twisted ideology, not a would-be murderer like the rapist. It is only if he ... any stirring of that and he would be away in an instant to confess to the priest who must have got great prurient pleasure from the nature of all those 'sinful' confessions of the time. The trick was to admit you were an unworthy sinner and if you begged god, that is the priest smug behind the grille, if you begged him for absolution for those 'momentous sins' you might be forgiven with due penance. Priests, the original quack therapists. The poor man, a victim of his conditioning, how must he have felt to be told that he was always second class, that he would be just about tolerated if he did all his penance and kept away from the nether regions of himself.

23

He finds Maribel in the forest bumping into trees, groping at the branches trying to make her way stumblingly deep into the undergrowth which is still smelling of the charred earth. How did she get there? Had she just wandered away from the villa on her own? Oh Maribel, where do you fit in the scheme of things? She is the pawn, the one who has suffered, and a tremble seizes him. Will he worsen her fate by progressing his own selfish desire?

He is about to speak, to call out to her, for he is wandering too, ascertaining in a perfunctory way the damage done by the fires, the state of the trees, trying to spot any new life springing up again from the rotted duff of the forest floor, the old surviving trees sucking the poison from the earth to make room for the saplings. He is about to call out to her, to warn her of that malignant-looking spiky branch overhanging her that could strike her as the fallen branch had done so disastrously to her eyes. Maribel. The word is silent on his lips for it is she who speaks first, not to him of course, of whom she is oblivious, for she has her back to him as she enters deeper into the forest, but to her Angelo.

He watches transfixed, as she disappears out of sight behind a great pine tree scorched half way up its bark. Her arms, her legs, will be all scratched. She is just wearing short sleeves and those flimsy cotton shorts and flip flops, and he, as the one despised for intervening but failing to save her beloved, does not know quite what to do now. He stands motionless until eventually her body disappears out of sight and it is just her voice becoming a faint echo calling on her lover until there is nothing left, not even the sound of a bird and, like someone defeated, he turns away.

***

He locates Auden's poem *Spain,* the original version transcribed by hand by Brother Marías into his mini-squared notebook, and which he had given to Paul before his trip to Spain 'so you will know something of my country from a non-Spaniard but still a man of insight'. Paul with his pencil underlines the polemical phrase 'necessary murder' in the context of the Spanish civil war. That was what the revolutionaries believed?

It is the early hours as he lies stretched out in his bed, the fan whirring overhead. Was Auden naïve or had he just used a wrong word, a poetical device, or did he really believe in the deed? Would he have killed a man for a belief, an ideology? The conscious acceptance of guilt in the necessary murder. But then that was only poetry and poetry, we are told, makes nothing happen. And besides, commissioned poems, which Auden's was, record merely simulated passions. He needs to rouse himself, to whip himself like those angry waves upon the crags, into a frenzy. Convert himself into an ancient Celt going into battle painted with woad.

He looks at the photograph of Javier cut out from the newspaper which he had pinned on his wall. Every morning up to this he had pointed his finger accusingly like a revolver at this man in the immaculate navy suit and wine tie and pure white shirt as if Paul had been rehearsing a major part, a Shakespearean role, of which Viviana would be proud.

But he knows now he cannot do such a thing. He cannot engender hatred towards this man.

And, as for Auden, was it really a just war as he would like to make us believe, a war that never ended like the old civil war politics in Ireland which never really went away, divided allegiance to the grave and now that is being continued by newer methods? Continuing generations seeking justice. Or is it mere vengeance?

The prostate answers, that most practical of organs summoning one back to the present. The Aubade rises. Will he return to sleep. Or will it escape him? The cicadas are sounding already. A slivery streak of light is stealing the night away.

***

'When my brushwork lets me down,' he says, 'it's...it just does not satisfy me. It's awkward and smearing and clumsy. Those clouds look more like faeces. It's just not delicate. I want it delicate.'

'Try the knife Pablo, the palette knife.'

'You think so?'

'*Sí señor*. The knife is an achiever, it can do things.'

But when the thoughts are teeming the hand is slow, captured or lost in an instant. What is it about Spain? he wonders. The colours, their flag, the red and the yellow, and those workers he had seen on the roads with their navy blue shirts and overalls, uniforms in a Francoist way, all the same, removing their individuality which of course is the purpose of uniforms. See them in the streets, manning drills or down manholes, their tawny skin allied to Helios but their individuality is gone with those blue uniforms. They are like locusts in the sea of traffic or bees humming, all the same.

She is standing in the doorway after her shower, her hair is dripping in dark sensuous ringlets, erotically damp, the white towel draping her like a lady from ancient Rome. She stands there looking out towards him demanding to be admired, a painting completed and framed within the architrave of the door.

'What is it?' she says noticing his frown.

'It's not working,' he says.

'Still?'

'Still. When I look at you standing there now, you are already framed and then I look down at my faltering sketches and they all fall short, every one of them. You see it's not life-like drawings I'm really after with their anatomical accuracy showing throbbing biceps and pulsing blood vessels.'

'So you don't want to dissect me like da Vinci, is that it?'

'Not in that respect, perhaps metaphorically. No, to me it is more than geometric shapes.'

'Eight heads tall for humans, eight and a half for gods.'

'That's all that differentiates us then from them I mean, half a head?'

'Can you see the cellulite growing?' she says raising her leg onto a wicker chair.

'It is fine. I don't want a photographic model.'

'Am I not better than a photographic model?'

'Of course you are, but what I am looking for is not a bland sameness. I want voluptuousness, classical, satiety.'

'My! Those words, Pablo. Those concepts. But what about the pleasure?'

'Of course the pleasure.'

In the bathroom he studies every pubic hair she has left behind her in the shower, intricately trapped in the grouting of the tiles. Like a forensic expert he considers the minute sloughed-off skin particles, the residue of her.

They lounge around after a long, languorous breakfast which Conchita served on the patio. Viviana, her ringleted hair still dripping pearly drops onto the blue tiles. She is holding her bakelite vapour cigarette on the ready awaiting its post-prandial inhalation. Maribel sits across the table, her orange juice unfinished, her head averted towards the sound of some bird singing, an excuse to continue the snubbing of her mother. Her father had dropped her off to give her a reprieve from the overpowering summer heat of Madid.

Conchita clears the table. Viviana sits at the pool on one of the loungers in her scarlet robe awaiting Paul's instructions. She looks forward to his visits now; she likes the pampering; what egotist does not? And now as the summer moves on, she feels, even if he is not making progress as he would like on the portrait, at least she is making progress with her designs on him.

Yes, she muses smiling out at him. She holds the prize he is after, a garden of infinite delights. She has the art of giving the honeybee pleasure. She will have him then.

And Maribel takes in his painting with her ears. She hears the gentle brush strokes like waves on the canvas; she hears the scratch of the palette knife, the finger smudging whatever part of her mother's anatomy he is working on now.

When Angelo appeared in the forest the trees changed, the foliage turned to bright stars and the bluebells chimed. And when she saw Angelo, her heart soared, for he was the most beautiful boy she had ever seen. He was too good for this world. That's what happened. He was giving all his love to her because he knew he was going to be taken away like his father by water and him by fire. And it was then at that moment of ecstasy that she wished they could become birds so they could fly above the sordid earth.

Maribel is learning to play music. Her father's doing, and she reluctantly agreed for her papá. She is learning with the two senses of touch and ear, but perhaps without the most important sense of feeling. Some famous mentor related to the great Segovia— no expense spared on guilt— a maestro, trying to inflame her with the passion of flamenco to resurrect her spirit, the sound of the guitar echoing through the marble halls, the notes transported out into the sunshine, her fingers on the strings guided, and then he plays, the maestro, and slowly she comes out into the pool area shouting, but no, it is not shouting. Paul knows it is singing. She is singing the *cante jonda,* the music which Conchita applauds but which she knows her mother hates, proclaiming to the world at all its cruelties. And it halts Paul in his work as Maribel continues in her singing, her chest heaving as she attacks the strings with a fury, the strong sensuousness of pain and grief and passion and agony so overpowering, and with her mother shouting again, that he has to turn and walk away.

***

He dreams her hair is sleep-mussed like the fisherman's net. The old net discarded by the fishermen on the quay at G—. Some of the better nets are being repaired by ancient women, he saw them there with strained eyes as they darned, wearing shawls in the shade of alcoves. The net that the fisherman had given to Paul in a sheen of fish scales and seawater was too far gone for them to bother with. But it holds a thrilling visceral fascination for Paul and he thinks of the loaves and fishes, the Bible and Jesus out in the deep, all these parables somehow becoming real to him by his holding of this net in its dripping saline, as powerful as the nets thrown by Vulcan and Candaules. So he will keep it there on his balcony to consider as more than a metaphor.

***

The quiet place they had discovered near the nudist beach lies among rocks too stony or treacherous for the hordes of bathers in their pursuit of ease and sloth and hired sun bed and soft sand to the touch and lenitive waves. That was all further down. But this was a quiet cove with primitive rocks to hide one from prying eyes, and the roar of the sea to be out of human earshot

'This is the place, Pablo. This is the perfect spot,' she says with little sudsy wavelets from the receding tide bubbling around her toes. Her toenails are painted scarlet to match the flaming robe, the colour of blood. He could die so easily here he thinks sitting by the Mediterranean. No need for any action, just expire after a couple of San Miguels sitting on a foldup chair to be subsumed by those ever-powerful waves.

'What do you think?'

'About what?'

'About this spot. Don't you think it is the perfect place.'

'For what?'

'To entice him.'

'Entice whom?'

She shakes her head in frustration. 'Javier of course. He is driving me mad, Paul. We have to do something about him. He is phoning me day and night talking about Maribel non-stop, tormenting me. Why don't they go away? Both of them. He wanted to keep her in Madrid. Now he brings her back here. Just drops her here. Expects me to take on the burden. They won't go away.'

She takes his hands in hers. 'So strong,' she says examining them and then looks imploringly into Paul's eyes.

'Viviana, I don't—'

'Shh,' she says. 'This is our lair.'

'Our lair.'

'Yes. You will be the big spider, and I will entice him. I will be at my most alluring, Pablo. He will be so surprised at my change of heart tempting him down here to rekindle our nuptial passion for each other. It is so easy to arouse someone when you know his every nook and cranny. So when he reaches his highest point, when I have him crying out—he can be loud you know at such moments— when he will be oblivious to all round him, the roar of the sea or the screech of the gulls will act as our chorus to cancel his petty squeak. Then from your hiding place from behind that rock over there,' she says pointing, 'you can throw your net.'

'My net?'

'It's a metaphor,' she says, 'a manner of speaking. And once ensnared the rest will be easy. You will hold him down with your powerful hands. And I will have the pistol cocked. What could be easier? And the sea can claim him, and let the fool be damned.'

She puts her arms around him, squeezes into him. 'And then you and I, Paul...'

24

Like Auden's Spain, he writes in his diary, the Bible got there before him and talks of a just killing. He has free will. That is a faculty that he has never really used. Allowing him to make a decision all on his own without any ethical hangups. Otherwise what is the meaning of being free? He has only just been released from years of bondage. He has the power now over his own activities. His own volition. It is rational and self-made. It is not Viviana who is calling the shots but him, his own individual self. He has the power to fuck up his own life, if one were to use such a crude epithet, if he so wishes. All those years with God was nothing more than a distraction. He has removed that armour plate of religious certainty.

Any action of his from now on will be an affirmation of his free will. What he really wants is human physicality. More than anything left in the world to him now. To lie with a woman. To make love to her. To complete the human cycle. He was always a man of honour and never did engage as some clerics did in furtive sexual acts. But the opportunity has now arisen. Great life is calling, the last gasp of the bee. Is the price too high? Life always has its price. Look at the Christian martyrs, what price did they pay? Their bodies pierced or burned in supposed ecstasy for the suffering Christ. The sacrifice of the flesh, always the flesh. But now it is the soul's turn. The sacrifice of the soul, something non-existent, something generations had been fooled into believing was really there: nebulous, ethereal nothingness.

He has had a lifetime of so-called spirituality enforced. The warring factions of Flesh and Spirit that Saint Paul warned about in his Letter to the Romans. But what of the spirit of the flesh? The spirituality in the erotic? Art in other words.

She insists on showing him another movie in which the husband is cuckolded.

'Don't you think that's awesome cinema,' she says afterwards. She is chewing gum and trying to talk like the young American starlets. 'Don't you think he's an awesome director?'

'A famous one, yes. I think I may have heard of him. His name slipped past me in the credits. Or is his name a mere medley of others which sounds familiar with just enough exoticism to win the ladies? Ziperilli or Zaparelli or something like that?'

'Fudoli,' she says.

'Him?'

'Of course, him.'

'Okay. But I was never too gone on those types of films. The hype was enough to drive one on I suppose in enforced adulation, almost like a forced faith one could say, being made to believe in things we don't feel in our gut.'

'You don't feel it there. You feel it here,' she says, and she touches his crotch with her left hand.

'Well...'

She laughs, noticing the bulge in Paul's pants as she withdraws her hand. 'When I met him first...'

'Who?'

'The director.'

'Benito.'

'Good. You got his first name.'

'When he first arrived, he told me he had been an unemployed script writer from Roma.'

'How they all wound up in Hollywood. Don't they have their own film industry in Rome?'

'Ha, Hollywood on the Tiber. The *cinecitta* there did not want him. His type of film, they looked down their noses on it. Condemned it. So he went to the real Hollywood to promote the film noir.'

'And that's when he contacted you.'

'Yes.'

'And you were married to the minister at the time.'

'Yes, but Benito had my old films and he was a man who was a rising force. He wanted me to go back to the silver screen. He had a part for me, a part that would make me immortal, don't you understand, like Monroe, Bacall, Hepburn. He had a major male star to play opposite me and I would be made for life if I accepted the role as his co-star. We would get an equal double-billing, and Benito had contacts with big names like MGM and Fox. He'd got them all interested in the story. But,' she sighs, 'time was running out, Maribel was growing, the taller she got the more I seemed to fade.'

'You're not jealous of your daughter, surely?'

She stares at Paul for a moment as if she is about to challenge his audacity, but decides to say nothing. She just turns her head to left and right as if in disbelief.

But the torment persists: that man Javier, he knows deep down is not bad as Viviana insists. He is not convinced and, without conviction he cannot act. How could he possibly accede to such an insane request, whatever the rewards? But maybe it is all illusional with Viviana. She got the idea of murder from the film noir. She is mixing up the real with the imaginary. She thinks she is acting out a film role.

Back at his apartment he realises he has forgotten one of his brushes. It is late when he returns to the villa. The gate is open. Viviana has grown careless. As he approaches, he hears voices coming from the master bedroom.

'You made the wrong move marrying him.'

The words in English, the accent Italian.

'I know that now, but we have the means of solving it, haven't we?'

'The part, I can only keep it open for so long. There are a lot of top actresses seeking it and some—'

'Younger than me, isn't that what you mean?'

'I didn't say that. It's a career-making opportunity.'

'I know. Oh how well I know that. Be patient, Benito. I am making progress with the old guy.'

'You promise?'

'I guarantee.'

'You know I still adore you.'

He hears their breathing. Are they touching? Is he about to kiss her?

'Patience, Benito.'

'Divorce him. It would make things so much simpler.'

He hears her tutting. 'I already told you, he will not accept that. He would fight tooth and nail. He would haunt me like he always did.'

'But the old guy, is he really that innocent and, more importantly, is he capable?'

'He is strong despite his age. He needs a little more training and maybe a little more convincing, that's all, and then I will have him like putty in my hands.'

'And that ruse, that painting he is doing of you?'

'He is quite good actually, but then so is the subject matter.'

'I know that *bella*, how I know it.'

With darkness drawing in, he ponders on his balcony on what he had overheard, convincing him that the object of his desire is a ruthless woman who is capable of anything. But she still attracts him. He can do nothing about it. He is like a magnet, unable to resist. Desire knows no bounds. The siren-enchantment of her curvature leads him on to what? His own perfidy, he is at her mercy. Free will, he has none, as long as she holds that authority over him. So now what difference does it make whether there is a Benito or not? He, the senescent innocent, at her beck and call, is a slave to her every wish, even knowing. Even knowing...

***

The next morning he makes no reference to the particulars of the previous night but, as he sketches, enquires cursorily about Benito Fudoli.

'Ah Benito,' she says making herself comfortable on the sunbed, 'let me tell you about him. He was born in Napoli of poor parents. His father was a brute who worked in a pasta factory. Benito ran away when he was still a teenager. He was a fiery kid and and had got into many a scrap on the filthy streets of the Quartieri Spagnoli before he came to Rome. He wanted to work in the film industry. He had seen films in the old reels in the rundown cinema near his home. It was his escape from the squalor of his existence.' She pauses. 'Like my escape too for a different reason. And he fell in love with the black and white film which the old proprietor Giuseppe used to show in his rundown theatre so few had little interest in. But he took a shine to Benito because he shared his interest in those films while others rushed off to the bigger cinema in the city with its technicolour and panoramic vision. But he and Giuseppe would watch those films together, all the film noir with Humphrey Bogart and Robert Mitchum and James Cagney and all those Hollywood legends. And he told him to go to America to become a great movie maker because he told Benito he had great ideas. But Benito went to Rome first to see would they take him on to work in their film industry.'

'You seem to know him very well.'

She considers Paul for a moment from under her eyes. 'Why would we not know each other well? We have shared the same interest in films for a quite a while now.' She stretches. 'Anyway they would not accept him in Rome. They did not like his southern accent. They told him to go away and get an education, and they wouldn't listen to his ideas, the million plots that he had hatching in his head.'

'You know about that, his plots?'

'What are you insinuating Paul?'

'Sorry I...'

'Ha. You are coming on, Paul, really coming on.'

Lighting her vape she continues, 'For two years he scraped and saved, working in restaurants and taverns near the colosseum in the Via Sacra licking up to tourists, hating every moment of it until he had enough money to leave the accursed place and take old Giuseppe's advice and board a plane for America. Ha, see Roma and die they used to say, well he had no intention of dying I can assure you. Not with a name like Benito, he would say, named after the greatest leader Italy ever had, and how they treated him in the end.'

'And you,' Paul says, 'you think that?'

'What, Mussolini? Of course not. But Benito was Hollywood-bound. To the land of dreams realisable. His suitcase was overflowing with a wealth of ideas and pitches and scripts written in the mode of the film noir. When he reached Hollywood he was sure they would listen to him.'

'And did they, listen to him I mean?'

She reflects for a moment. 'A few did, but most of them said the film noir was an out-of-date genre.'

***

On his balcony looking out at the sea, he hears a delivery van arriving. There is some noise of goods being delivered to the local store and then the noise fades, He looks at the card Javier had given him. He had ben twirling it between his fingers. He phones the number. A female voice answers. 'The minister is not available at the moment. Could I ask who is calling?'

And then in less that five minutes, the call back. 'Yes, my friend, I am free now.'

A half hour later they are sitting down at the corner table of the same restaurant where they had met before. 'You want to ask me more about my wife. She was the desire of my heart. From childhood. From schooldays when she was crowned the little orange blossom queen in our village. And I remember in a school play she put on a blond wig and did a few wiggles like she was Marylin Monroe, driving the boys mad. In class I used to sit at the back desk in awe of her, daydreaming, staring, being scolded by the teacher for not paying attention when I was looking at her all the years of growing up. I just could not take my eyes off her as she developed. I could see her breasts forming, her legs lengthening, the uniform becoming too short, so deliciously short, although I was not quite able to explain why she showed me disdain. But I licked up this disdain like nectar discarded by a goddess as her curves were forming, doing I did not quite know what to my still uncomprehending prepubescent mind.'

He stops and sips his coffee. 'Forgive me my friend, for such an outpouring. I needed so much to confide in someone.'

'That is okay,' Paul says.

'A goddess.' He sighs. 'She was a goddess to whom I would always be enraptured. You must admit my wife is truly a treasure to behold. I don't mind admitting it, no matter what the circumstances. Viviana's beauty was known to all the village, but you see my friend, in all the time there was one thing I did not know about Viviana, blinded as I was by her beauty. We all get blinded by that, my friend, don't we?'

'What was it you did not know?'

'Well...' His brow furrows. 'Her mind was weighed down with too much stuff. Her father...'

'What about him?'

'He overloaded it. Fed a poor girl's brain with too much from art and literature. Made her very dissatisfied. That is what her father bequeathed to her, a great dissatisfaction with her world. His own dissatisfaction with his humble status he foisted onto the daughter. So she was never at ease and always had these *anhelos*, you understand?'

'Yearnings,' Paul says.

'Yes, but more than yearnings. An endless seeking to be someone else, someone better, someone more important. It started off with headaches. The problem. Strong headaches which led to worse things as time went on into our marriage.'

'What sort of things, if I may ask?'

'Outbursts towards me and later Maribel and even Conchita. Sleeplessness and delusions, most of all delusions. Oh yes, such delusions she had. Her trouble, my friend, was she could not live in the world as it was around her, the real world.'

'The medication,' Paul says, 'did that not—?'

'Oh,' he says, 'you noticed the medication, or medications. All those bottles and phials don't always work. She just kept taking them and I was worried that they could become addictive, and when I would enquire about them she would just say, "Doctor's orders". That runt-sized doctor of hers coming and going without a greeting like a horse blinkered, he is another one she has twisted around her finger under instructions never to divulge what exactly is going on for years now between them. Oh don't think I didn't try to find out what he was diagnosing and prescribing. I stopped him one day. I was polite to him. "Good day, señor," I said. "I am the husband of Viviana" even though I knew he knew that as well as knowing I was a minister. After all I was in the public domain, so how would he not know? But despite being aware of all that, he persisted in trying to walk past me. And I blocked his way so he was forced to stand still. He looked not at me but away to the side and seemed most uncomfortable as he drummed his fingers on his thigh. "Can you tell me what my wife...?" and before I could continue, he spat out the words like it was clockwork. "All matters between my patient and myself are strictly confidential" and he snapped the catch shut which had become loose on his leather satchel as if to end the matter.'

Javier stops to regard Paul. 'It is a sad state of affairs, don't you think my friend, that my wife has enjoined her doctor to silence even from her own family?'

'But notwithstanding,' Paul says, 'you had your own career to deal with as minister, your own ambitions.'

'They were fortuitous, my friend, not by design. The Cortes is just a place to hammer out laws.'

Running a hand across his head, he adds, You see my father was a politician pretty high up in Franco's government and yes, maybe with a blemished reputation which Viviana and some others are not slow to remind me of. But that was in the past, soon after the civil war when people did things which perhaps they would not do now. All I can say is he was a good father to me. So I just drifted into the tradition. Although once in it, as I said to you before, I did work hard. But it was always Viviana I went home to. Even now she is the one. Despite treating me badly. It is the price. I accept. The price an ugly man must pay for a beautiful wife.'

'Hardly ugly,' Paul says.

'Oh yes, especially after the accident. I knew she wanted to part from me then. But I am a Catholic. I believe in what God has joined together, in sickness or in health. She was sick too, her mind and my leg.'

'And all this started, this infatuation, as far back as when you were in school together?'

'What has she told you? No, don't tell me, probably that I kept pestering her for I and, it seems you too my friend, if you don't mind my being so bold as to say, have fallen under her spell. For let there be no doubt about it, she did weave an irresistible spell on any male who was weak enough to fall under her sway, and indeed I was weak enough, that weakness, what is that weakness but a succumbing to the beauty of the female form? We men can do nothing about that. We are cursed.'

'You really believe we are cursed?'

'I do. And she is my undoing and to this day is still my undoing, for I can do nothing about it. She is like a drug, a narcotic that no matter how much damage she does to me I find impossible to give up. A curse to bear in hindsight and you my friend,' he says staring at Paul, 'you may rue the day you first set your eye on the alluring charms of Viviana García del Alonso.

25

Early morning session. Yes she did ask him to come early this morning, saying that she wanted to talk to Paul, and there was an urgency in her voice as she spoke to his cell phone.

The scent of jasmine is wafting somewhere by the pool. And notwithstanding what she may wish to do, he positions his easel slanted to avoid direct sunlight.

Sitting on a wicker chair in a silk kimono she is cast downwards at the blueness of the pool, the little ripple in the water from a gentle breeze whispering through the cordylines.

'So,' he says.

'Don't talk,' she says.

'What is it, Viviana?'

'The gadfly. He has become pathological, you understand, I don't know how he conducts his work in the Cortes.'

'To do with the fires?'

'The deaths that were caused by them. They are blaming him. The way he is handling things. Some are calling for his resignation. His party have dropped in popularity. You surely have seen it in the papers.'

'I'm afraid I wasn't paying much attention to the media in the last few days. So what will Javier do?'

'That's why I wanted to talk to you Pablo, when we are sharp, bright and early. The people saw through him like you and I? You did see through him, didn't you in your brief encounters with him? Tell me you did, Pablo? Tell me you saw through him. Pablo?'

***

It is late morning, when Señora Mendoza knocks at Paul's door.

'There is a chauffeur waiting for you.'

'Thank you,' Paul says. He hurries downstairs past the bemused landlady to the waiting car half guessing who it is.

'I have to talk with you, my friend,' Javier says as Paul sits into the rear seat of the black Audi, noticing Javier's dark glasses. 'I hope I haven't inconvenienced you at this time.'

'No,' Paul says, 'it is a good time.'

'Have you eaten?'

'Not yet.'

'Perhaps we could have lunch.'

'Same place?'

'Yes.'

He gives instruction to the chauffeur, the same guy who had picked Paul up the previous time they had dined. The driver coasts along as they head towards the hills, as if his slow pace is deliberately compelling them to take in the burntout houses and trees and blackened earth and the source of the fires.

'It is so sad, is it not, for those people who have lost their homes?' Javier says. 'The opposition are blaming us, our party and me, as minister, in particular, but I am doing all I can to help them.'

'I'm sure you are,' Paul says suddenly feeling that was not the right thing to say, that it could contain an underlying sarcasm.

'And even more worrying is something else.'

'What is that?' Paul says.

He nods in the direction of the chauffeur. 'I will tell you,' he whispers, 'in the restaurant.'

The restaurant is not very busy and they manage to find a quiet corner.

'I will phone my chauffeur when we have finished,' Javier says. 'He is a good man but inclined to gossip, so I have to be careful what I say in public.'

A tall young waiter as slim as a toreador appears with menus.

'I am not very hungry after all,' Javier says, 'just soup for me.'

'Soup is fine,' Paul says, without even enquiring the type. 'So what is it you want to tell me?'

Javier scans the restaurant. When he is satisfied there are no diners within earshot, he says, 'The matter of the cigarette lighter.'

'What about it?'

'We are both implicated, she and I, but the letters V and J could have belonged to a thousand people, couldn't they?'

'I suppose they could.'

He takes a white handkerchief from his trouser pocket to wipe the beads of sweat which have formed on his brow. 'It's just the niggling you know.'

'Niggling yes. I can understand that,' Paul says. Niggling, yes that is the word, all those things that niggle one in life. Always there, always something niggling.

'It won't go away. It won't let me sleep, particularly with Viviana prancing about at all hours. Thankfully there is no surname. Just: To V from J.'

'From you?

'Yes. It had been a birthday present. Oh to think that I also could carry a blame for the state of my daughter and,' looking towards the window, adds, 'those poor people out there.'

'You cannot blame yourself for that,' Paul says.

He regards Paul as the waiter arrives with onion soup in earthenware bowls.

'You are a good listener. That is a quality of a true friend. But you must forgive me, I have asked you hardly anything about yourself, how your painting is going...?'

'It is going okay,' Paul says.

'You must find it strange, my friend, this family of ours.'

'Well...'

'She is becoming impossible. She has probably spoken to you, I mean about me.' He is whispering as if the walls are conspiring against him. 'She has poisoned you against me, no?'

'Well, she did say some things.'

'You don't have to tell me,' he says waving dismissively with his serviette, 'I know already. But let me tell you, my friend...' He draws closer to Paul '...I wasn't the dumbo she tries to make me out to be. I was bright enough at school in a quiet way, not in the flamboyant way of Viviana. I was good at Latin and history and I got a *beca*, a scholarship you understand, to study politics in the university of Almería. I was good in political debates and later in government for a sort of staid safeness, a good party man who wouldn't rock many boats. This man won't stun but will get the work done, a steady workhorse, just what is needed now after the turbulence of the past. Our history, my friend, as I am sure you are aware, is bloodied. But that is what they said about me. A safe pair of hands, yes. And indeed, if I may not sound too boastful, I did excel in that role. I lost myself there in the middle of a harangue, had no hangups, no emotional fragility. I was robust, a warrior, an apologist for a new Spain. Although there is much opposition now over the fires. I have to deal with that. And I would have been able to do it,' he says with growing emotion, 'difficult and all as it was, were it not for my weakness, my Achilles heel.'

'Viviana?'

'Always Viviana. I could break down in her presence if she was unkind to me. I was at the mercy of her moods, for I adored her and that adoration was like an affliction. And no one in my political circles knew about this, for the country considered Javier de Alonso as a robust politician. But all the time I had to look over my shoulder. I never knew what she was plotting or scheming, and half the time I would let things go, thinking it was to do with those half crazed plots of those silly films she was always watching. And when I would be organising the photos for the press I never felt comfortable. I would be always neurotically checking on her, checking that that lascivious Italian producer was not around her.'

He reaches for his pocket in his linen jacket and takes out a cigar which he puts back again as soon as he has taken it out as if it is some error. 'She could've been a good wife only for him. She did appear to enjoy at least for a while the political limelight, and I thought she would be happy with that, she would settle down, and that was the way our lives would pan out. But there was always the spectre of my father which she never lets me forget.'

'You carry your father on your shoulder through your life,' Paul says.m

'Perhaps, but as I have said he was always good to me and I try to be a good man. I try to look after Maribel. It is an open secret what my wife thinks of me, but you see señor, I loved her despite her ways. I loved her since childhood, since we shared the same classroom in our local school. We were meant to be together. You can't go against the stars. The stars dictated it, but she tormented me. I have no hesitation in telling you, my friend, she taunted me in front of others, she lifted her dress for boys to leer. They queued up behind the bicycle shed and paid centimos or toffee bars to behold her legs, and the only condition was they were all obliged to say how beautiful they were which was easy to say as it was true. And I was one of those boys. But while other boys as they grew up moved elsewhere in their infatuations, the image of those legs stayed with me and she entered my soul.'

'You believe you have a soul?'

'Of course, on the last day...'

'I know all that,' Paul says dismissively.

'Indeed, I forgot you were in the religious life. Viviana had told me in her pretence to put me at ease about you.'

'At ease?'

'Yes, but there was no need now that I know you as my friend. I knew there was no danger of dalliance and there was the age difference of course.'

Paul hesitates. 'Javier I...'

'No no no.' He touches Paul to silence and says, 'Not that it would have made any difference I suppose when you consider all the others she had dalliances with.'

'There were many?'

'Oh yes there were many but none like you my friend, none of them venerable like you.'

Paul knows his use of the word *venerable* is simply a polite euphemism for *old* or even *innocuous*.

'Yes. But let let me tell you about my dear wife. She was a female of great beauty and great intelligence. She got higher marks than most of the boys in the exams including me. And her father, the status-seeker, sent her to Cambridge. Could you believe that? He wanted her to be better than all the rest of us. It was a very competitive class I must admit. But she never tired of mocking me, and the more she laughed at my prepubescent pimples the more I swooned for her and continued my pursuit of her as my destiny.'

He scratches his balding crown. 'Have you noticed how she flaunts herself and gesticulates endlessly despite the frown she may carry. A man-eater or a man-killer, what is the difference?'

'A man-killer, you say.' Are these prophetic words Paul is hearing even though he believes they are not literal in the mouth of Javier.

'Oh yes,' Javier continues. 'She can turn it on when she wants. Surely as an artist you must have noticed her altering moods my friend, like darkness and sunshine.'

'Yes.'

'She can look like an angel or a seductress, whatever is her whim. She's an actress remember. She can do all the parts.'

He takes out his cigar again and starts to tap it up and down on the table. 'Can I tell you something about her? When she holds your arm which I am sure she has done, have you noticed it is not a caress but a controlling grip? You may be painting her, Paul, but she is directing the brush. And may I tell you something personal?'

'If you feel...'

Javier is silent while the waiter appears to remove the soup bowls. And then in a whisper continues. 'After we would have sex you know when she was satiated what she would do...'

'Javier you don't have to...'

'She would kick me out of the bed, physically landing me on the floor like a lump of mutton. I have no hesitation in telling you my friend, we were on a turbulent sea and I always tried to steer a straight course, but you know the story of Ulysses, you know the sirens. I know what draws you to her, my friend. I have seen the way you look at her, and I take no offence, for it is the way many men look at her and I have got used to it by now. And I have seen some of your sketches that you left behind in the villa. And they are good, they are very good.'

'Thank you,' Paul says.

'But let me tell you, to dampen your ardour of that mystical pilgrimage you are on, her derriere to be precise is not all hers.'

'What do you mean?'

'I want to put you straight about her. You are an honourable man. You saved my daughter's life. It is only right that I tell you the truth about my wife before, like others before you, you fall prey to her wiles, before it is too late.'

'What are you saying?' He is growing impatient with the minister's roundabout way of speaking.

'What I said my friend, she had buttock enhancement, implants señor, gluteal augmentation to give it its proper title. What the Hollywood producer insisted on her having for the coveted role. Would you believe it? I opposed it of course, that interfering with nature. Besides she was already beautiful. I told her that. Why alter something that is already perfect to my eyes at least? But they insisted, those people in Hollywood. For the new part. They thought her derriere had flagged a bit in the photographs Fudoli was showing them of her and based on her previous films, and she would be required to show it off in the new movie, a brief and tasteful, oh yes that was the phrase, a brief and tasteful nude flash.'

'Could they not have got a double,' Paul says, 'I mean — '

'No, señor. She wanted, she insisted and they agreed. She wanted all the glory if that is the word. And think of me, my friend, my career with a wife degenerated into profligacy for all the world to see. So I threatened, and the threat still holds, that I would let the world know.'

'Is this really true?' Paul says.

'Oh yes. She swore me to secrecy. She wanted to be sculpted into an aesthetically pleasing shape. For me, but I knew it was not for me. It was all a lie, señor. It was her producer she was doing all this for, the new film. Don't you think she was too perfect to be real? Smoking, hot, seductive, they were the words the producer would use for a femme fatale, or fatal because her beauty could bring about the death of her men.'

'You are just talking about the films, surely.'

'Oh señor, she wanted to be the greatest femme fatal of all time, better than Davis, Hayward, Stanwyck, Stone, better than all of them regardless of the consequences. Oh she would dream about it, cry out in her sleep, pester me, wake me up to talk about it non-stop into the early hours. She would torment me about those actresses into many a dawn hour. Even when I was troubled and wanted to talk about the fires, she had no time to listen. But I was happy for her if she wished to act here in Spain in our *patria* without going to far flung fields. But she was not satisfied. She wanted far flung fields. She would do anything señor, to achieve that ambition. I suffered in all humiliation. Any man she wanted, I turned a blind eye to, because I could not lose her. And now my friend, even you, if you don't mind my saying so, are not in the prime of youth, I fear what she has in store for you. Fatal,' he says pronouncing it in the Spanish way, 'you know what it means? It means decreed by fate. She was destined to be that way as I was destined to be always her doormat.'

'But you could... I mean you are an eminent politician.'

'Ah my friend, you have heard of Socrates. A beauty's kiss is deadlier than a spider's venom. No, I should have fled but I stayed and now I am her slave. And Viviana is still a beauty even if it is artificially augmented. People call her a Venus, but they don't know that Venus was a slaughterer of husbands. She commanded every woman on the island of Lemnos to murder their husbands. And they, as if they were hypnotised, complied. *Cave amantem* beware of love, señor. She is too beautiful to be bad. That is what they say, especially the men, and she knows it and uses that beauty and delights in her badness. And we are powerless before her. But the people of the village know her. They have long memories and, with the death of the local boy, there is anger among them, señor, great anger.'

Paul notices the waiter eyeing them from a distance. The restaurant is quiet with just the mumble of a half dozen people talking low at well spaced tables.

'Do you think we should order something else?' Paul says.

'*Dos coñac*,' Javier shouts towards the waiter. '¿*Vale*?' he says to Paul.

'*Vale*.'

'In school,' he continues, 'I was jealous of her giving the other boys those thrills. I wanted her all to myself but she would delight in hurting me with her scoffing. Even at that young age she was conscious of her power over the male. She missed school a lot more often in secondary than in primary. We never learned as kids what was wrong with her. Viviana is sick, that is all the teacher would say. I was very upset. I missed her so much. I would look over at the empty desk as if my soul was empty. She had to spend time in hospital. It was only later, after we had married that I learned of her mood swings and depressions.'

He presses at some particle caught between his teeth.

'No, it wasn't the body that was the problem. She was attracted to her father, very close. You know he had a great influence on her.'

'Yes, I had gathered that,' Paul says.

'He told her things about men.'

'Did she tell you what they were?'

'No so much, more hinted at over the years.' He pauses. 'I had to have her committed once.'

'Committed?'

'When things got out of hand. She never forgave me.' He glances down at his legs. It was during the second year of our marriage after Maribel was born, the train crash happened. No doubt she told you about that in all its gory details.'

'Yes.'

'I suppose I was lucky to survive. But you, my friend, can see the state I was left in. But Viviana could not accept that she was going to have to spend the rest of her life with a cripple. She would attack me physically, flaying with her fists. Can you imagine, as if I hadn't been damaged enough. She even tried to shoot me once.'

'Shoot you?'

'Yes when I was at my lowest ebb soon after I had come out of hospital. You would think it would have been the opposite, that she would have sympathy for me, but no, nothing but scorn. I was lying on the couch watching the television when she came in and pointed her fancy pistol at me. And, only for Conchita intercepting, she would've killed me, I am sure of it. Perhaps it was due to the medication she was taking at the time, I do not know, but only for Conchita...'

'So you had her committed.'

'I had to. What choice did I have, señor? Either that or prison if I had pressed charges. Neither Maribel nor I could tell what her next course of action would be. She never liked the child, I was thinking of her safety even more than my own.'

Paul looks around. Just a couple of tables are now occupied. Middleaged couples engrossed in their own worries, broken by the odd laugh.

Lowering his voice once more he says, 'She spent nearly a year in the sanatorium in Madrid. She is on different medication now, but I'm not sure what they are. As I have already said her doctor tells me nothing so I do not know what lies she has fed him about me. I have to keep an eye on her all the time. She could explode at any moment like a time bomb. But you, my friend,' he says as the trace of a smile removes the seriousness from his face, 'I must thank you from the bottom of my heart for allowing me to speak so frankly, so intimately to you.' He clears his throat. 'You, as someone from a different country, can bring an objectivity and an impartiality to this conundrum that I find myself in. You allow me to speak my mind without fear.'

'I am honoured,' Paul says, 'by your trust.'

'For the truth is there is no one else I can trust. In politics it is all ulterior motives. Friendships are forged not on sincerity, but on opportunity.'

'I understand,' Paul says.

'But let me tell you, with Viviana, there is no one person there.' He sighs, 'Never was. I mean who could satisfy her?'

'Fudoli?'

'Ha. Yes, he keeps cropping up, doesn't he, filling her head with unrealisable dreams. But you, my friend are a pure man, almost like a holy man if I may say.'

'I don't know about that,' Paul says, 'if I am all that pure or holy.' And his mind wanders to señora Mendoza saying something similar and he wonders is the cloister so ingrained in him like a slate that he will never be able to wipe clean?

'But tell me,' Paul says. 'Why do you think she wanted to kill you? Was it because of the accident?'

'That yes, the fact I was maimed was repulsive to her, but she knew I had something on her.'

'The enhancement?'

'I threatened to reveal it when she expressed a desire for a divorce. But she could not divorce me, it was not possible. I threatened that I would expose her, that the world would learn what she was really like, that the goddess was no goddess but a woman of clay.'

26

It is late evening as he watches Maribel feeling her way towards the edge of the pool. Viviana has withdrawn to her bedroom and he has gathered up his easel and canvases and brushes into his cotton shoulder satchel. He is about to depart when he hears her plop into the water. She makes no effort to swim but just lies there face down inert, the outstretched arms and the long shape of her under the blue luminosity of the water, and her hair like seaweed floating. 'Maribel,' he calls. But there is no sound or movement from her. He straddlejumps into the pool and pulls her out. Laying her on the edge, he pumps her chest and administers the kiss of life.

Her eyes open and she smiles as if she can see him. She asks if there is a bird in the room.

'No bird,' he says. 'And we are not in a room. Maribel are you...?'

'Oh no, not you again,' she says, recognising his voice. She cocks her ear. 'There is some sweet sound but not from you.'

Conchita appears coming out of Maribel's room carrying a steaming bowl of vegetable soup on a tray.

'She will not eat. I tried to coax her.'

'Leave her, don't coax her,' Viviana snarls, made up now in her pencil suit. 'She will eat when she is hungry. She is being stubborn just like her father and,' turning to Paul, adds, 'Conchita says Maribel is now self-harming. She cuts herself, her arms her legs, that is why we have to keep knives and cutlery away from her. Isn't that right, Conchita?'

Conchita lowers her eyes. 'Sí señora.'

'Oh the wild ways of adolescence,' Viviana exclaims.

'She nearly drowned,' Paul says.

'Playacting, that's all it was.'

'But señora...' Conchita is standing hesitantly with the soup.

Viviana glares at her. 'What did I tell you?' And then rising, to Paul more suavely, 'And now I must go. I have an appointment.'

Paul gently pushes open the blue door of Maribel's bedroom. Her bed is small, her toes are exposed and overhanging the end base, as if her bed has not been changed since she was a little girl. She is sleeping now with rather heavy breathing. For some reason he thinks of Snowwhite, the little bed with the sky blue duvet and beside the bed on a little table a phial like the phial Viviana had given him, and a silver frame with a photograph which she can no longer admire of the boy Angelo Machado smiling out with his coifed hair and shining white shirt, an angel indeed even if he did smoke weed, and on the floor he brushes against a skateboard with the wheels removed.

***

Although Paul has grown fond of paella, the following evening in *La Cuchara* he pushes the yellow turmeric rice to the side of his plate.

'You're not finishing it.'

'Not really hungry.'

'You sound like a child.'

'Perhaps,' he says.

'You are still thinking about my daughter.'

'Yes, I mean how could you...?'

'What! You're going to tell me about the non-swimmer saving the drowning girl. Spare me please.' And then taking his hand she says more gently, 'Look Paul, don't fret yourself about her. Her father will look after her. The two of them you know are like this,' and she joins her forefingers together like a chain.

'Your appointment or should I call it rendezvous went well?'

'Ha, all this prying, old man. Funny, how you have lost your bashfulness together with your appetite. I don't like that. I prefer my artist bashful. It is so not in keeping with the general perception, don't you think?'

'You care about things like that?'

'Why not?'

'And what other things do you care about, Viviana?'

'What's this, a trick question? What do I care about?' she says arching back and gazing towards the high ceiling. 'Freedom,' she says. 'I care about that. Personal freedom,' she clarifies, and what I don't care about is something or someone who tries to take that away. In your case Pablo, it may have been the church, am I right?'

'And in your case?'

She sighs, one of her long histrionic sighs. 'What is one to do with something deformed? The more he tries to touch me in fact the more repulsive he becomes. I don't mind telling you this. I don't care anymore who I tell. And the increasing whining voice about his struggles in the world of politics and the expanding paunch and the baldness growing in ugliness you might say.'

She scans Paul's face. 'Whereas you Pablo, despite your years, still have a trim, an unmarked body. And your eyes are so beautifully blue and fresh. Did anyone ever tell you how beautiful your eyes are?'

He doesn't answer.

'You are pristine Pablo, coming to me straight out of the factory. Oh, and another thing I like about you...'

'Oh.'

'Unlike others, you don't try to possess me.'

'Do I not with those eyes you like so much?'

'That's because you think I'm beautiful.'

'I do?'

'Well then don't you know, a beautiful woman always needs someone else's eyes to validate her beauty.'

He excuses himself. The prostate has been troubling him in recent days. In the lavatory staring at blue tiles it is a slow process, like his painting he thinks, this relieving of one self, slow and painful, waiting endlessly for the last drip to finish.

'What took you so long?' she says in a cut-edge voice on his return. She is puffing furiously on her ecig enshrouding her in a pall of smoke. 'You think I have nothing better to do than wait on you.'

'I am sorry, Viviana,' he says, 'I...'

'You know who I am? Do you really know who I am?' She reaches such a high pitch that Paul fears she may get a heart attack. 'You can't treat me like this. It is not right.'

'I said I was sorry.'

'And now,' she says rising, 'I am not in the mood for you.'

The next day he is early, making a point to arrive at the villa five minutes before the customary appointed time of eleven a.m. The French doors are open and a slight breeze is ballooning the muslin curtain outwards. He is about to enter when he hears Viviana's voice on the phone.

'Not now...Not till I have enough... no no. It will be sorted. I promise you. I know the cost but I need a little more time. I am sure. Yes. No, Don't. Stay where you are. Maribel is attending a psychiatrist. No no, of course I am not attracted to him. It is you. Only you, you know that. I merely have to pose for him, yes just posing, nothing more, the slightest curvature on my part and his prick stands up to attention like a soldier obeying the erotic order. Ha ha yes.'

She hears Paul's gentle cough, a deliberate clearing of the throat. 'I will phone you later.' A surprised look from Viviana as she turns around. She places the phone down, the look dissolving into a smile. 'Ah Pablo, you are on time today. Good good. Let us commence.'

Lying languidly on the sunbed she says, 'What is the size of your canvas?'

'Three feet by two.'

'You Irish and English say feet, but I understand. I am taller than that.'

'That may be, but the world is taller than you,' he counters.

'What? Are you annoyed with me, Paul?'

She rises and approaches the easel. 'Let me see what you are up to. Is that nose as yet undefined?' Peering over his shoulder she exclaims, 'What have we here? A man on a crutch, a girl with a white stick, a sleeky haired man exiting a side door. And to the left a man with a white beard looking on. What is this, Paul?'

'Experimentation. Sorry,' he says fumbling to find a fresh canvas. 'I had been sketching on my veranda.' And he thinks of his sketching odysseys in the monastery and how like a writer's pen his brush is telling a story.

'But it's supposed to be just about me, and you of course the artist. Isn't that what you want?'

'What about Benito?' he says.

She baulks. 'What did you overhear?'

'Enough.'

'What does that mean? Enough for what?'

'Nothing,' he says.

'Let me tell you something, Paul. Benito is giving me an opportunity, a last throw at the dice to save my career, you understand?'

'And what about Javier?'

'You are jumping from one man to another.'

'Isn't that what you do?'

She looks away into the distance. 'Javier wants to certify me. Did you hear me?'

'I heard you.'

'And you say nothing.'

'He wants to have me locked up. Have me locked up. Like your institution, Pablo, only worse, a madhouse. That's where he wants to put me. He and his daughter are in cahoots against me. He wants to commit me as he did once before, branding me as a person of unsound mind. It is a lie, isn't it Pablo? I want you to tell him it's a lie.' Her look towards Paul becomes a commanding stare. 'You will tell him.'

'I will tell him what you said.'

She puts a hand to her forehead. 'What does that mean? Oh, all this arguing, all this stress, I am not able for it. It brings on my headaches don't you know.'

'I am sorry,' Paul says, 'I didn't mean—'

'Can you fetch me a glass of water from the kitchen fridge?'

'Of course,' he says glad of the opportunity of a reprieve.

The Paralympics are showing on a small television set which is perched on a high shelf in the kitchen as Paul pours water into a glass. He nods across to Conchita who is watching the programme intently while standing at the worktop filling a fruit bowl.

Swimmers in blackened goggles are moving fast down lanes to the encouraging shouts of people with various degrees of disability: paraplegics, quadriplegics, athletes with impaired movement, amputees.

'*Mi hija,*' Conchita says.

'Your daughter,' Paul says, 'which one?'

'La parapléjica que está ganando.'

'She is winning. But you could've been there with her,' Paul says.

'Not permitted, the señora...'

'Perhaps your husband...?'

'*Muerto,*' she says.

'What is keeping you?' Viviana shouts bursting into the room holding her head with one hand and her ecig in the other. 'What are you two conspiring about?'

'We are watching Conchita's daughter. She is swimming, winning actually...'

'Turn that off,' Viviana snaps.

Conchita turns off the TV and exits from the room in silence.

'They shouldn't put on programmes like that,' Viviana says turning to Paul and, still with the bitterness in her voice, adds, 'It's not natural.'

'Not natural?' he says.

'Those people, they should not be taking part in sport. They should not be allowed.'

'So what should they do?'

'They should be hidden away. It is pathetic,' she says snatching the glass from him, 'to have to look at them.'

He is in a sweat. He has to excuse himself to go to the bathroom. It is not from the heat that he is overcome but from the onslaught. Conchita's daughter treated with such scorn. Does Viviana not realise her own daughter Maribel, formerly a good swimmer herself, disallowing that unfortunate incident, could she aspire now to be among the ranks of the black goggles? Could she compete? Was it not laudatory if she or any disabled person could try to live in the world? Would her mother frown on that? Or has she just assigned her to institutionalisation to be forgotten, the thing she is supposed to have feared herself, to be proscribed like he had been for so many years? He had never thought of Paralympics before. He was familiar with the term, but for Viviana to pour scorn on such people has unbalanced him. Poor yes, he had encountered plenty of poor people and undernourished people in South America and even in Ireland. It was the Ignatius Rice mission statement after all to care for the poor, but there was no mention of disabled. Why did she have to bring that up?

He looks down at the trickle of blood in the bottom of the bowl, but passes it off, fearing she will be complaining again of his toilet delays. And yet, coming out of the bathroom seeing her slowly moving towards the pool, her robe discarded, he is drawn no matter what she says, no matter how obnoxious the utterances are spewing out of her mouth, that snap at the maid or the waiter, that denounce people who are different. This is the same mouth he was only yesterday trying to capture on canvas to turn it into art, as if it were its own entity, a different organ separate from the beautiful parts of her.

27

He will consult Javier again. He finds the card. No answer from the landline. He tries his mobile. 'You are fortunate my friend,' Javier says answering, 'I am just on my way back from Madrid.'

They meet in a café near the harbour with the coloured fishing boats bobbing up and down expectantly where their conversation can be drowned out from prying ears by the sound of men's dominoes.

I no longer share the matrimonial bed,' he says. 'God knows who she shares it with now.'

Paul budges uncomfortably. 'You think she is...'

'I know her, my friend. She always has to have someone in thrall. It is her way. But anyway, tell me how your painting is coming along. Don't you find my wife a great poser?'

'That is one of the reasons why I wanted to talk to you. I wanted to find out more about her. If she dislikes her daughter so much, why did she say she was beholden to me for saving her life? Why did she offer to pose for me as a repayment?'

'Not as a payment my friend, but as a vanity, so she can admire her own image whether in celluloid or paint, it's all the one to her.'

'Let me order some coffee,' Paul says.

'*Café solo*,' Javier says. He takes out a cigar from his linen jacket and starts to roll it between his finger and thumb. 'Viviana lies,' he continues. 'You discovered that yet?'

'Yes, I...'

'She will say anything to suit her mood in her relations, she will tell you things, my friend.'

'I am grateful to you for meeting me, Javier, and also grateful for your openness. It is unusual if I may say for a husband to talk so freely about his wife.'

'It was not always that way. One can be driven.'

'I understand.'

The waiter, tall with a white pinny, delivers the coffee.

'Knocking sparks off each other, that is the phrase yes, that is what we do, although it is mainly she who does the worst damage, but never severing, going on and on in a life of slow mutual destruction. I am thinking of giving up politics.'

'But not the marriage.'

'I have already told you...'

'Yes you have, and I am sorry to hear that about your career.'

'The strain is now becoming too much especially with Maribel the way she is. I felt so guilty leaving her. She is a disturbed child. I want to give time to her. And besides, you probably know our party lost a confidence vote in the Cortes over our handling of the fires. I did my best in that regard but I'm afraid it was not enough.'

'And the personal cost,' Paul says.

'Yes above all, that. Maribel is more important to me and will always be more important to me than politics.' He laughs. 'What do you think my friend, two cripples minding each other, eh?'

'You are being harsh on yourself.'

He stops rolling the cigar. 'I turn to you, my friend with this sorry state of affairs.'

'I don't know if I can be of any help,' Paul says and he thinks of Viviana's injunction not to let Javier have her committed.

'Did you ever read that book,' Javier says. 'It was popular in translation here many years ago but I always refer to it, by the American Bishop Fulton Sheen *Three To Get Married?'*

'I heard of the bishop,' Paul says.

'That's what's needed in a marriage, a third party as an arbitrator, and that arbitrator is God, señor. But you know the problem is she won't let Him in. She lets on to believe one day and the next day she is an atheist.'

'The actress.'

'Yes the actress, and if you challenge her veracity she will twist words around. I am a politician, Paul. I understand the nuances of words. I know her ways.' He crushes the cigar in his fist. 'But it all got too much. She's become too much.'

'Desperation,' Paul says.

'Exactly the word.'

Javier rakes his fingers across his dome as if trying to find a lost part of himself. 'You know she would never admit this to you, but Viviana used to look to me to protect her when things got bad, like I was a well-worn cushion. When she couldn't cope, she would always come back to me and phone me every day. But she forgets those things now. And when I would talk about yesterday, the things she had said, she would say who cares about yesterday, it is all about today, our lives are of the moment, the past and the future are illusions.'

'The mood swings,' Paul says.

'Popping her uppers and downers, but what really keeps her going are her plots.'

'What plots?'

'To threaten me. To threaten my life. It is a step too far. That is why I am trying to consult with the doctor to have her ...'

'Committed?'

Javier takes in a deep breath. 'Maybe we should have a little *coñac*, my friend, to add to the coffee.' He summons the waiter.

'I could explain to that doctor the threats she makes to me.'

'Continues to make,' Paul says.

'Oh yes. That doctor who comes and goes, Doctor No Fuss as Viviana calls him. That dour, taciturn fellow. I have discovered something about him. Viviana let it slip in one of her tirades. He is not only a medical doctor. He also claims to be a psychiatrist. Both of them were hiding it from me of course, for she was afraid I would use it as ammunition against her. She tried to get him to counsel Maribel also after the fires, but I would have none of it.'

'You don't think it would have helped Maribel?'

'No señor, not by a quack like that. I arranged for Maribel to be counselled by a reputable person in Madrid.'

'I see,' Paul says.

'And don't you think, my friend, it would be the safest thing for all concerned?'

'You mean to have her put away?'

'No no, not put away, just to have her cared for, to escape her plots, until she gets better. Don't be fooled señor, she has ulterior motives for you too.'

'When did these plots as you call them start?'

He places the cigar with its torn leaves in the glass ashtray. 'Soon after we were married they started. But maybe they started before that with others. Who am I to tell? Instead of feeling joy, my wife resented it when Maribel was born. She showed no affection for the baby. It was a mistake, she said, too early, and it interrupted her plans. Conchita of course was wonderful in looking after Maribel. So the disgruntlement soon set in. She said I was a jinx. You understand the term.'

'Yes.'

'After the train crash and then Maribel's accident, she said I brought her nothing but bad luck.'

'That accident must have made a huge impact,' Paul says lifting his *coñac* in its tiny glass

'It wasn't the accident that changed things, bad and all as that was, I mean in our relationship. She would have put up with me. No, it wasn't that. It was when she met Benito Fudoli who promised her the sun the moon and the stars, and she in her vanity believed him. When she had, as I thought she had, hung up her boots, and after a short stay in the sanatorium.'

'The sanatorium?'

'Just a few months was all was needed to get her on the right track again, to calm her down in her desire to take on what I considered the more significant role of wife and mother. But then she got the phone call. I remember the night very well. Maribel was not even one at the time and she had the colic and was crying and she wouldn't stop. It was in the middle of the night and Viviana cursed her for wakening her, for she had been in a deep sleep as she often is after her medication. She gave me her customary kick to get up and see to the child. And I walked the room with Maribel in my arms up and down for over an hour singing softly, soothing her until I calmed her and got her back to sleep in her cot. And when I returned to our bedroom Viviana was sitting straight up in the bed holding the phone with a big grin on her face.

'What's the grin for?' I said for I was very tired and wanted to get back to sleep.

'Someone still wants me,' she said fully awake. 'An Italian director. 'See, I'm not washed up, not like you, *cojo*.'

28

'Just say... a crime of passion. The old guy is in love with me. He will do what I say. It will be so simple... of course... to be rid of the gadfly, he will no longer be in my hair buzzing around, making me....we will be fine. No no, I told you, don't come yet. No, do not change anything. There is no point, that I assure you. Yes, I know you hold the... there is nothing to worry about. Maribel is blind yes, it is definite. She did not recover. Yes, I know she doesn't approve. She never did. I cannot alter her opinion of me, not now. I know, I know they are waiting and growing impatient but you darling, with your charms can stall those fat financiers. Yes I know he is a famous actor and it is great you got him, yes and I will be delighted to co star with him, but stall, stall, it will be worth it. I am grateful, of course I am grateful. I won't let you down. It will be a...'

A sound. Paul with his easel at the French doors waiting, a brush falling on the tiled floor.

'...I have to go.'

She glares at Paul as he stoops to pick up the brush. 'Would you please knock at the glass in future when you call. You startled me.'

'Oh I startled you, did I? Tell me who is the old guy?'

'What old guy?'

'That you referred to on the phone. I overheard. Is it me?'

'Of course not, Pablo. It is a character from the film that I am hoping to make.'

'I am growing to like your company,' she says as he returns after a thought session in the bathroom.

'Only now,' he says, surprised that she is not tetchy with him as before on his delay.

'Especially now,' she says appearing relaxed on the sunbed. 'I enjoy our conversations. They are of a higher quality than the average dick.'

'Who is the average dick?'

'Men.'

'Men? Are we not all individuals, gender neutral?'

'Ha ha,' she says, 'I really do like your mental processes. There is a logic like a Latin grammar to your thoughts. I wish I could think like that, logically I mean.'

'But there is a logic to you,' he counters. 'You flatter me while trying to hide your secrets from me. To put me off the scent as it were. Isn't that it, Viviana?'

'Oh no, Paul,' her voice mellowing. 'There are no secrets between us. Don't your realise you have become my confidante, my mentor. If you are referring to the phone call...'

'Yes I am referring to that.'

'That was just my director trying to get me back acting.'

'You never stopped acting, did you, Viviana?'

'Oh Paul, don't be like that. Don't be like Javier. You are listening to him too much, all his lies. He has contacted you again, hasn't he?'

'We have been in communication.'

'In communication ha, that's him talking through you. Political talk. Did you tell him?'

'Tell him what?'

'Oh Pablo, don't you listen to me at all? What I asked you to tell him, that what he is insinuating about me is a lie, all lies.'

'Are they all lies, Viviana? I am beginning to wonder.'

'Stop it,' she snaps, putting her hand to her forehead, 'you're bringing on my headache.'

What she has planned, the sex with Javier; she knows like all men he still craves her, and she will pretend (the actress coming out in her) for Maribel's sake to put a brave face on it. But all the time the injustice of her fate will be festering inside her. She is a seductress, a femme fatale. She will tell Paul how she will use her skills at seduction. She will not cringe. She will allow him to make her feel repulsed. She will sweet talk him. She will no longer mock his lameness or his baldness. She will say, No more animosity for Maribel's sake. She will try from now on to please her husband, and you Pablo, good trustworthy Pablo, will be waiting behind the rock for the signal when he cries out as he always does when he is in the throes.

'Oh Viviana what are you asking me to do? If I were to help you to kill this man, your husband, this gadfly as you call him...'

'There is no need to fear. It is I who will be doing the deed.'

'But I would be an accessory. You are asking me to hold him down while you... are you aware of the consequences? I will go to prison. Is that what you want? You care that little for me.'

'Of course I care for you.'

She approaches to touch him. He withdraws.

'You will use your wiles to which I am enslaved as you surely know by now and then compromise me so you can escape with your darling Benito.'

'No Pablo, that is not the plan exactly.'

'*Exactly*. What, you want some modification, is that it?'

'I mean we want to make it look like Javier did himself in.'

'We?'

'Yes we. We will let the sea claim him. I mean after that train crash he was never the same, and then there was the backlash from the fires and now his daughter's tragedy with no hope of her sight returning, it is the final straw for him.'

'The final straw maybe for me as well. Perhaps it's your plan to get rid of us both.'

'Will you listen. You will await my instructions. On our quiet strand he will not even see you, Pablo. He will have his back to you. For all the world to know he will have stridden into the sea with a pistol to his head and go to the other world not knowing who sent him there.'

She takes a breath to regard him alluringly. 'And now, Pablo,' she says approaching him once more, 'I am upping the stakes.'

Despite his conviction she is mad, the dropping of her gown is like the sea tide sucking him in. Drawing him by the hand she leads him away from his easel and, not giving him time to wipe the paint from his hands, lays him down on the sunbed. She mounts him. She taunts him when he is at his highest point of passion. She withdraws asking him again for his answer. He is left panting like a dog, his tongue out and his eyes pleading. She turns. 'The way you like it,' she says, 'but first an answer.'

'Whatever you want, but please let us finish it, please.'

And what was it like, that moment? In the act did his life rush before him? Did all the sublimations coalesce and sink to nothingness, fall to dust? Did the vacuum in his life fill up? Did he feel complete at last? None of those things. Where are the other facets of himself? A moment of frenzy, was that all it was—what he had missed out on all his life? Was that it, a mere moment of pleasure, albeit excruciatingly wonderful carnal pleasure, but ending so quickly like a puff of smoke? And what is he left with? Something longer-lasting, the recompense, the bargain, the deal, *upping the stakes*, selling his non-existent soul to a truly existent Faust. He will have ruined his life. He will have sold himself out. But if he can renege on one ethic, surely he can also renege on another, the ethic of a promise. After all, it is not a level playing field that he finds himself on. Viviana cannot be trusted. He has established that she is a liar and he a mere pawn in her plan of things. Does she really believe that he would buy into the idea that she cared for him, this old guy, and would continue her relationship with him after the deed is done, while the director of all her dreams is waiting in the wings?

29

In the church of San Pedro.
The attributes of the Virgin.
The lily.
The rose.
The palm tree.
The mirror.
The orb. The crescent moon.
The serpent.

He is sitting in a pew—no more kneeling, he will never kneel in a church again. He concentrates his gaze on the altar as he battles with his conscience, and the tabernacle he remembers in a poor barrio in San Salvador, the little chapel of Santa María. He was sheltering from a storm and the same woman who lost the baby sneaked in. She did not see Paul in a side pew in a dark part of the nave and she looked around her once or twice and checked the golden door of the tabernacle which was open— the padre must have forgotten to lock it. She took out the hosts and, concealing them inside her blouse, walked down the aisle and out into the storm.

'What are you doing here?' Viviana whispers sitting beside him veiled in black. I had been looking for you everywhere to put the final touches to our plans. I have it all clear in my head now. Conchita said I might find you here.'

How did Conchita know, he wonders. Ah yes, he remembers asking her for the directions to the church.

'Pablo.'

'Keep you voice down,' he says. 'You realise this is the church where the funeral took place. The boy...'

'Don't you think I know that. It is of curiosity to me.'

'Curiosity.'

'Churches have some practical benefits, don't you think,' she says upbeat now looking around. 'The dark interior, the cold stone, the black flags, all exude a coolness. Was that how they won them in the hot countries, the converts?'

Detecting his sigh she says, 'Ah, it makes sense that you are in here after our consummation. You are here to seek affirmation, isn't that it, Pablo?'

'Affirmation?'

'For the deed that lies in front of us.'

'How can you say such a thing in a church?'

'Because our deed will be a just deed, Pablo. Remember you promised.'

He doesn't answer. How cold, he thinks, how cold her eyes are?

'You will never shake it off, will you?' she says noticing his gaze on the the cross hanging over the altar.

'Shhh,' he whispers noticing the disapproving look of a supplicating señora in a nearby pew. 'My eyes have gone green from looking at that wood. It makes me tremble.'

'Still?'

'Just like the wood must have trembled under Him, don't you think. *Bajulans sibi crucem exevit.*'

'What is that? Some sort of chant?'

'*Carrying the burden of the cross to himself he went out*. We were meant to share that burden with Him, and that sharing was original sin.'

'But we don't think like that anymore, do we Pablo?'

'What you ask me to do...'

'What we agreed. An act of liberation. But now you are consulting with your boss, is that it?'

'No, it is with myself I am wrestling.'

'You are strong, Paul,' she says, putting her hand on his broad shoulder. 'You would have made a good wrestler.'

'The problem here,' he whispers, removing her hand, 'is there is no room for other points of view. How can we be branded with a sin that we did not commit?'

'You are talking of original sin, I take it.'

'Yes. It accounts for all our human guilt. How could one ever be happy by subscribing to such a belief? You're doomed from the word go.'

'They promise the afterlife, isn't that the consolation?'

'If there is such a place, and if it's supposed to be sought after with such fervour, why do they frown on suicide, which is the fast-track way to get there?'

'You think suicide is the fast-track way?' She muses. 'Maybe there is—'

'Is what?'

'Something in what you say.'

'Sorry I'm...'

She sniffs. 'Pablo there is a smell of incense here which is overpowering.'

'They must've had benediction.'

'Whatever,' she says. 'I need fresh air.' She rises and he looks after her, her hips swaying iconoclastically as she fades into the darkness of the church, and a shudder seizes him for the walls seem to grow colder with their heavy stone makeup, as he rises to follow her.

'What I was thinking,' he says as they come out of the church, 'was not just about what you are asking me to do.'

'No? I thought you were in there trying to bury your conscience.'

'No, it was more than that, Viviana. It was about my whole life that wavered before me. The fact that I never really made any big decisions in all my life, it is easy for the likes of me to say I am a moral person when I have never been tested. How can you say you are moral when you do nothing?'

'You did save Maribel. That was a moral action surely.'

'But that was unthinking, spontaneous' (and he ponders, like his action in San Salvador). 'And now if there is no conscience, as you would have me believe, just as there is no soul or original sin, which is something I figured out for myself sitting there in that pew— Can you believe it? It took all those years to figure that out. Just now. So if there are none of those things, what the heck.'

She laughs. 'Yes, what the heck.'

'But...' he hesitates, '...that phone conversation I overheard unsettled me.'

'There's no need for that, I explained, did I not...?'

'Would you really throw me in a heap, Viviana, when the deed was done?'

'Throw you in a heap, what a phrase.'

But he is not at all convinced either morally or strategically of her plan. What man would walk into the sea with a gun and put a bullet in his head to commit suicide? And even though she claims he would just have to hold Javier down while she plugs him, he would still have to lift the body seawards, and the bullet could surely be traced by discriminating lawmen to her pearl pistol. The more he dwells on the implausibility of it all, the more convinced he is that she is truly deranged.

'What you are implying,' he says, 'is that our action, were we to engage in it, would be a moral action too.'

'What's the difference, Pablo, between saving someone from a fire and saving someone from themselves?'

'Wait.' He stops. 'You can't possibly equate the two.'

'Don't you understand, you will be giving me back my life and your reward, I promise you, will not be in heaven but on earth. A world of earthly delights awaits you, my handsome older man.'

'How can I believe that? Listen to me, Viviana.'

She starts to mimic a Beatles' song which he recognises, '*I showed you once before. I can still show you some more...*'

'Viviana.'

She continues to sing, silencing Paul and, as he goes to interject, she sings louder. Then as as they turn a corner into the main street of the village, she stops and, removing her veil, looks up at the darkening sky. 'Look at the ringed moon. It has come out to greet us. Just look at it, Paul. That is how we should look at the world, we should look at it and judge it slantways, don't you think? Like the moon sees us. Who is to tell us how we should perceive it?'

'Perhaps we need a darkness to comprehend.'

'Yes.'

'Like your Caravaggio but...'

'But what?'

'Without the violence.'

'There has to be violence, Paul.'

'I'm a sketcher,' he says ignoring the jibe. 'I can draw you now from the source of my unconscious.'

A dream. Hundreds of sketchings and lithographs and paintings in oils and acrylics but never finding completion knowing that the Big Fellow is the only competition.

'I will have you know,' he says, thinking of the pearl-handled pistol and its possible corollaries, 'I am not into violence.'

'Does your word not mean anything, Paul?'

He ponders. He never broke a promise in his life, not that he made many: at his confirmation yes, and to be true to his vows yes, but ah yes, the promise to the celibate life, he broke that.

Eventually he says, 'Do you really think that a promise exacted in such a manner—'

'What manner?'

'You know what manner. Do you really believe such a promise can be binding?'

'Oh Paul, a promise is a promise no matter what you say.'

'Viviana.'

'No no,' she says, turning her head from him. 'You are becoming tiresome now Paul, with all this ethical nick-picking of yours. Was what I gave you meaningless? I gave you myself. What more can I give?'

'I am grateful for what you... for what we...'

'Oh Paul.'

'Let me put it to you another way. That Caravaggio whom you appear to venerate is not really my cup of tea as a person.'

'Ha, you and your tea. He is a great artist, Pablo. I love him: his violence, his unpredictability, his fearlessness, all those qualities.'

'You don't need a shady past to be an artist. The violence you subscribe to is the violence of emotion.'

'Really? You know me that well?'

'The only thing that will satisfy you Viviana, is to see John the Baptist's head on a platter with the blood oozing.'

'Yes, I rather like that painting. But it is not John the Baptist I am after. Give me Herod or Judas, then you would have him.'

'Him?'

'But the head oozing,' she muses, 'it will be messy'.

'You are acting. I know you are acting.'

'Am I? You flatter me.'

'All this fabrication comes from your films. I think I understand you now. You are not really asking me to commit murder or even assist you to do so. You want to simulate it. You want me to play a part, act out a role. The career that was stopped before its time. You want me now to co-star in your movie to pretend to kill a man.'

'Ha, you think it is a pretence.'

'There you see, it is you trying to satisfy some unfulfilled longing inside your twisted self.'

'Oh I'm twisted now, am I? Whereas before...'

'It's all makebelieve, isn't it Viviana?'

She hums the tune again.

'Stop that humming?'

And her mockery irritates him just like the pigeon foraging in the nearby litter bin with its monotonous cooing.

So engrossed are they in their argumentation they do not see the uncle Antonio approach more like an apparition, the fiery weather-beaten face with its two day stubble. He is upon them as they draw near the harbour, his eyes intent on Viviana as he wields his fish knife in his left hand and slashes outwards, slicing down the left side of her cheek with the experienced fisherman's thrust.

It is too late. Paul steps between them but it is too late as blood gushes from her cheek, and she holds her hand to her face in disbelief. She does not scream. Hers is more like a low ululation like the old women weeping on the death of their local boy.

And then the uncle's voice can be heard as he is pushed back by Paul. 'That's for Angelo,' he shouts. 'You come here among us. Have you no shame?' And some old women gather like a Greek chorus. 'She thought she was beautiful. Too good for us. Better than a killing.'

30

In the hospital in U, the same building where they had brought Maribel, there are queues and people on trolleys still suffering from the effects of the fires with different degrees of burns: old women and wizened men and young children wrapped in bandages. Bandages are in short supply, he hears a nurse say, let her take her place in line with the others, no special treatment here in the frenetic rushing about, and here is this film star now demanding attention. Javier arrived immediately after Paul's phone call, leaving Maribel for what he believed to be her own safety in the villa with Conchita. And Conchita, whom he also phoned, how taciturn she was on receiving the news, showing no emotion on the demise of her mistress. Was it possible that she, if her dislike of her mistress was so great...was it possible that she had tipped off the uncle that Viviana would be in the church at that time? She would certainly have reason to feel odium towards her mistress, judging by the way Vivina had treated Conchita and her daughter with such utter contempt over the years. Conchita could have walked, but jobs were hard to come by and Javier had persuaded her to stay. But the draw for her was always Maribel whom she had cared for since she was small, so small as a baby, often left by the mother crying in her cot, a small helpless baby not so different from her own daughter at that stage of development, until later that is when her heart nearly bloke to witness, not formation but deformation, in the direction her baby was going.

Paul tries to banish such thoughts and concentrate on the present as he sits in the waiting room anxiously, and there is Javier sitting beside him trying to keep a brave public face. For there are those who recognise the politician. And they throw desultory looks in his direction wondering what is he, the minister, doing for us as they think of all the people who have died in the forest fires. They eye him accusingly or murmur, their disapproval doubly evidenced in the brusque manner in which the hospital staff treat him when he enquires about his wife. And Paul wonders what he must be feeling inside—genuine horror for his wife's dilemma or maybe a feeling of quiet satisfaction that this image she had coveted all her life is now no more.

Paul waits. People need time. Husband and wife, he is drawn to both in a strange way: Javier for his honesty apparent and Viviana, despite all her madness, for what she must be going through. There is Javier now enquiring solicitously after his wife from the doctor and nurse. Despite Viviana's disavowal he must still have feelings for her or empathy or pity, the word to be wary of. Paul was there too when the stitches were put in and again when they were removed several days later —the cut too deep for dissolvable stitches— and horror, the deep intake of breaths, as the big glaring wound unfolded and Paul ghoulishly wondered if perhaps there had been some residue of fish in the blade of the knife: a halibut or cod. What a thought to have as pity soared outwards ironically despite the waning of such emotion.

From his balcony as night falls he sees the slatted blinds of the villa drawn.

***

Pressing the intercom at the gate, on a bright morning of the eight day after the assault, Conchita answers.

'She can't see you today, señor.'

'But I...'

'I am sorry.'

He hears a cry. It is Viviana, a half shout coming from her room.

'I must go, señor.'

The following day the gate opens immediately to his announcement and he finds her on her sunbed by the pool looking at herself in a mirror.

'Are you feeling any better?' he asks, noticing the scars a couple of inches slanting down her left cheek.

'Better,' she says continuing to stare into the mirror, 'better than what?'

'Better than yesterday.'

'Yesterday. What was I yesterday but an old coat, and the day before was I better then? She treats the word as if it is a sour pip in her mouth. 'Or the day after,' she says, 'maybe the day after I will be better than the day before. Or the day now for ladies with mental problems, for rest cures, as if I'm not resting enough here by the sea. You can vouch for me, can't you, Pablo? You can have a word in their ear. In the meantime I have to pose for you, don't I? Which cheek would you like to leer at today?'

And Paul wonders is she too distracted to vent her spleen on Conchita who was instrumental in her going to the church in the first place. Conchita comes and goes now without so much as a word from Viviana. Or more than sarcasm, why does she not hurl her spleen on Paul himself. She has gone inward. Too far gone there. Her mind is no longer capable of finding scapegoats.

'The mistress is acting like a *niña*,' Conchita says as she encounters Paul coming from the bathroom.

'She is growing increasingly sarcastic with me too,' Paul says. 'It is understandable I suppose after what happened.'

'We all have our tribulations, señor.'

'You don't feel sympathy for her?'

'We all have our tribulations.'

Paul hesitates and then says, 'I hope you don't mind my asking you Conchita, but the evening I went to the church did you... tell her where she would find me?'

'But of course, señor. She was very anxious to meet up with you that evening, like there was something urgent she wanted you to do. She kept muttering to herself, 'Where is he when I need him?'

And Paul thinks maybe it could have been Fudoli she was needing. In which case the dreadful encounter with the uncle could have been avoided. But maybe Conchita knew that all along. Maybe her directing Viviana was wilful planning.

'Did you not realise,' Paul continues, 'there would be people in that area who did not like your mistress, I mean especially after what happened to Angelo?'

'People are entitled to their likes and dislikes, señor.'

'Yes, I suppose they are,' he says, deciding not to pursue the matter any further.

Paul asks Viviana if she intends pressing charges against the fisherman who lacerated her face.

'What would be the point of that?' she says. 'More torment, that is all it would bring. Let them jubilate in their little village if that is what they want to do.'

'I would still like to paint you,' Paul says.

'Ha,' she says, 'to make a laughing stock of me. To join with all the others in bringing me down.'

'No, I don't wish to make a laughing stock of you. Surely you know by now that is not my purpose, Viviana.'

'What is this art of yours,' she says kicking with her left leg, 'but a demeaning of woman?'

'No, Never a demeaning, more an apotheosis.'

'Ha, some apotheosis.' She picks up her mobile phone. Benito, I keep phoning and texting him but he will not answer. What is it with *majos* when beauty fails?'

'You are still a beautiful woman, Viviana.'

'Ha,' she says, 'only in the nether regions now for dirty old men.'

So it came down to that in the end. She showed her true colours. He was just a dirty old man, a lecher, one who leers, that's all she really thought of him. It took the slashing to bring out the true thought of her many selves. All the acting, all the entertainment, is it over? And he wonders about her homicidal plan which she never mentioned since the assault. Is it to be abandoned or merely put on hold? He will not ask out of fear.

So what will he do now? Will she welcome him anymore, and the painting so nearly finished? Will it now change direction, or what is to become of it? Especially now when the subject has lost its allure for him.

Dawn has not broken. It is still dark and Paul is restless. He cannot sleep. He goes to his balcony and watches some late-night revellers cavorting down at a pool. And up towards the hills the black of the earth and by the light at the villa he can just make out two *guardías civiles* approaching the intercom. Is it to do with the uncle, or have they found out something incriminating about the cigarette lighter and the fire? And he sees Viviana looking out from behind her slatted blinds, her face drawn, as if she is trapped in the final scene of a film noir.

***

She is missing, Conchita says when Paul calls next morning. She is not in her room

Paul goes to the beach, the quiet place, the ideal spot where the plan, the 'just deed', the act of liberation, was to be carried out. The whiff of danger propels him spontaneously as it had done previously to the forest fire and the swimming pool. And here he is now in the quiet place. It is still early morning. There is nobody about, no sound except the gulls squawking and of course the sound of the sea. He walks towards the waves. Something catches his eye, a fish, a scale, offal from the boats perhaps but no, the bulk is larger, ballooned, looming before him. He wades, indifferent to the water soaking through his shoes.

It is Viviana lying face down in her black bikini being ruffled by the receding waves (her 'enemy' waves). And, as the sun rises, he catches, through the trace of crimson, the pearly glint of a pistol in the shallow water.

31

Maribel is now attending the blind school and lives with her father in Madrid. The father has retired from politics, his resignation accepted by the prime minister on humanitarian grounds.

Paul visits them, an invitation from Javier. When he gets off the train at Atocha station he is immediately enveloped into the overpowering heat of the city's late summer. He is surprised to be met by a smiling Conchita waiting on the platform in an attractive black laced dress (the black surely wasn't for grieving, more for joy perhaps or in keeping with her Andalusian heritage?) She is to direct him to the rendezvous. 'Yes señor,' she replies to Paul's enquiry, 'the master asked me to continue working for him, to help him with Maribel, and of course Maribel herself wants me. 'And,' her eyes light up as she adds, 'he has given me permission to visit my daughter anytime I wish. Isn't that wonderful, Don Pablo?'

'Yes Conchita, it is indeed wonderful.'

The Alonso apartment is near the Retiro and it is there in the Paseo del Prado he meets Javier with his daughter. Maribel no longer with a stick but with her specially trained guard dog, a fluffy cream-coloured Labrador. She calls out, 'Angelo', and Paul looks around as if the ghost of the boy will appear, but it is the dog she is addressing.

Paul is not sure as Maribel is drawn away by the dog, what to say to Javier on the death of Viviana. To express a shock or mutual relief or merely to sympathise, to offer condolences? For what? But when he sees Javier, despite the heat of the city, still wearing a black mourning tie, he offers his hand wordlessly. 'Thank you, my friend,' Javier says clasping Paul's hand in both of his. 'Thank you for coming. I know what you must be thinking. Believe me I understand what's going through your mind, that my wife was no good and perhaps you are right. But she was my wife and I must keep reminding myself of that, and I have to work on Maribel also and try to convince her of her mother's good points.'

'How did she take to it, her death I mean?'

'If you think it affected her badly, then you are mistaken, my friend. When I told her her mother had died, she didn't even enquire how or under what circumstances. She just shrugged and said, "What's new about that?" There was nothing, nothing between the two of them other than a vacuum, or maybe a cauldron of poisonous vipers, who is to know for sure.'

Javier looks closely into Paul's eyes as if pleading with him. 'She was my wife, no matter what. You must understand that, my friend. It is only right to grieve for one's spouse.'

'Will you be all right?' Paul says.

'We will be okay, Maribel and I. We will survive with the grace of God. The trick is to keep our selves in check. All the different parts of us.' He sighs. 'That was the thing Viviana was not able to do.'

And Paul thinks, yes, Javier is still a relatively young man, young enough to marry again, if he were to wish, to have a new life. But on second thoughts, knowing him for his faithfulness in matters of the heart, it is unlikely such a thing would happen. He is a man who will be faithful to the memory of his wife until the end of his days. And looking at him now with tears of grief still welling, Paul knows he cannot tell Javier that the woman he adored was planning to kill him.

Yes, Angelo is the dog's name. It was the psychiatrist Maribel attends once a week who suggested she call him that. Her trauma appears to be easing, judging by the calmer way she now conducts herself, an acceptance perhaps dawning slowly on the inevitability of her condition. This suffering, the psychiatrist told her, she will accept and use it for Angelo and she will be happy with that, believing she is fulfilling a purpose now, making progress with the Braille, and her beloved papá sacrificing his career to be with her. She is not *loca,* at least not in the way some of the villagers maintained, although they were sympathetic to her because of her tragedy, and they vented all their spleen on her mother. If she had brought her daughter up differently, if she had been a good mother, if she had been there for her to advise and help her, instead of flitting off in her own fantasies.... And that fellow who saved her, that *forastero,* she must not blame him. He just thought he was doing good, and she wonders— she meant to ask— when Papá invited him to visit if he ever finished the painting of her mother that he seemed to be so obsessed about. But the conversation was mainly taken up about her welfare: how she would cope, what plans were made for her, and the best she could do was bid him a gentle farewell.

***

Back in the old village of A—, Paul stands with the Vieja by the grave of his mentor and friend Brother Marías, loved beyond words, missed beyond measure.

He makes a hole in the sandy earth with a small trowel to place the Robinia to which previously he had given a good drenching, making it easy to slide with its roots intact out of its pot.

'You are going to plant it,' she says.

'Yes, a plant your son gave to me.'

'The robinias are plentiful in these parts,' says the Vieja recognising its genus. 'I have seen them in Tarragona lining the *rambla nova* all the way down to the sea. When María was young...'

She is holding on to Paul's arm. She is so small and delicate, and he notices a tiny white flower blooming on the Robinia and his heart gladdens, and he thinks how like the flower itself she is.

A warm breeze ruffles the feathery leaves.

'That's him,' says the Vieja, 'that's him waving at us.'

It is late autumn when Paul sets out for Dublin. He makes his farewells with Señora Mendoza who seems genuinely saddened at the departure of such 'an honourable gentleman' whom it was her great pleasure to be acquainted with. She expresses the hope that whatever it was the noble señor was seeking, that he found it in ample proportions in this land, which must have appeared strange to him in all its facets. But most importantly she hopes that he found, in whatever his undertakings were, true peace of mind, for surely that is the most important thing of all that a person can possess.

Frost and cold weather await him and shortening days and the prostate growing more painful, the plane journey, the seat constriction he blames it on, the letter from the Mater hospital still lying on the kitchen table. The PSF, the cancer progress form he never filled up, all in time, plenty of time at last to consider our mortal state. He now has something to look back on, rather than always longing. That longing is sated now, so he is happy, well at least content, to deal with matters in hand. And, as he opens the letter, he gives a little shudder on seeing outside, the ice give way to a drizzle, and he thinks of Helios, in a distant land, shining on the smallest twig.

About the Author

James Lawless is a novelist, poet and short story writer who was born in Dublin, Ireland. He is particularly interested in literature as works of art, aesthetically pleasing, and which throw light on the human condition. James has broadcast his poetry and prose on radio in Ireland and Spain, and he pens occasional book reviews for national newspapers.

His awards include the Scintilla Welsh Open Poetry Competition, the WOW award for fiction, the Cecil Day Lewis Award and the *Sunday Tribune/Hennessy* and *Willesden Herald* award nominations. His stories and poems have appeared in journals and anthologies including The Stinging Fly's *Let's be alone together*, and he was twice shortlisted for the Bridport Prize. He received an arts' bursary for his acclaimed study of modern poetry, *Clearing the Tangled Wood: Poetry as a Way of Seeing the World*. He divides his time between County Kildare and his cottage in the mountains of West Cork.

Printed in France by Amazon
Brétigny-sur-Orge, FR